Escape to Big Fork Lake

Mary L. Ball

Published by Inspired Romance Novels
First Edition, 2012
ISBN-13: 978-0615618265
ISBN-10: 061561826X

Published in the United States of America
http://www.inspiredromancenovels.com

This book is a work of fiction and any resemblance to persons, living or dead, or places, events or locales is purely coincidental. The characters are the product of the author's imagination and used fictitiously.

DEDICATION

"Trust in the LORD with all thine heart; and lean not unto thine own understanding." Proverbs 3:5 (KJV)

Dedicated to my husband, Joey, for supporting me and being my biggest fan. To my daughter Heather, the best daughter and sounding partner anyone could have. And to my cousin Karen, whose encouraging emails help me along my way.

CHAPTER ONE

Sam stepped away from his embrace and took a deep breath. The musky scent of his cologne danced delightfully around her nose. Her entire being longed to hang on to the peace that spread within her every time she was with him. Nevertheless, she knew it wouldn't last. "Goodbye, Bo, I'll see you next year."

Bo lingered beside his car door. As he stood in the parking lot of the sandwich shop, he studied Sam's face intently. He longed to make her understand him better. Perhaps if he lived closer, then things would be different.

Reluctantly, he opened the door to his vehicle. "Samantha, I really hate to go, but four hours is a long drive and I should get on the road. I really enjoyed the time we spent together."

A grin formed on her face, although she didn't like her formal name. Bo would use it sometimes. Gently, she scolded, "Now Bo, you know I want to be called Sam."

She watched him silently, mentally tracing the lines on his sun-kissed face. A sigh rode on her breath. "I'll see you the same place next year, Bo."

His brake lights glared as he turned the key in the ignition. Then, with a roar of the engine, he pulled into the heavy traffic and out of her life—at least for another year.

Sam crossed the street. Frustrated, she kicked at a stone and fussed silently. Again, she had forgotten to get his phone number.

The time they spent together was such a few short hours. She was happy just being with her good friend and reluctant to break the spell with questions of his other life.

She shuddered and pulled her jacket close. The cold, stiff wind seeped into her bones and numbed her skin.

Sam paid no attention as it billowed and tossed her hair across her face.

Walking faster, she rounded the corner to her apartment. She did recall Bo was a widower and he commented about living somewhere in Alabama.

One year later...

Sam sat at Baker's Sandwich shop and stared out the window. Since she last talked to Bo, so much had happened in her life. She couldn't wait to see him. If anyone could help her, she felt in her heart Bo would.

Her mind drifted back as she recalled the day she met him.

She'd taken a late lunch because of a big sale at the book store. When she walked across the street into Baker's Sandwich Shop and sat down at the counter to order a salad, the man seated beside her instantly drew her attention. Although he was older, something about him stood out. She couldn't understand why, but somehow his presence created a sense of serenity.

The slightly gray-haired man stopped eating and smiled at her. Just the glow on his face lifted her spirits. When he turned toward her, it was as if he knew what was in her heart. Intrigued by him, she smiled.

He nodded and said hello. Then he told her his name was Bo and that he was in Atlanta for the restaurant convention.

The next thing she realized, she was talking to him as if they'd known each other for years. That day when she left Baker's, she knew in her heart Bo was a special person.

When he asked her to meet him at the same place the following year, she eagerly agreed.

Sam shook off the memory and huffed out a sigh as disillusionment settled heavy on her shoulders. It only added to the cloud of despair that already covered her. She desperately needed to talk to Bo.

Sam was still upset about yesterday. She'd visited the police station and complained about her neighbor Rob in the hopes they would help her.

The officer apologized, saying that until her neighbor actually outright threatened to do her bodily harm, there just wasn't much they could do.

The policeman did tell her that if he attempted to force himself on her then she could charge him with harassment or assault and take out a restraining order.

She still didn't understand how a few simple dates could get her in so much trouble.

Sam rubbed the wrinkled lines of frustration on her forehead as she glanced at her wristwatch again and took one last sip of coffee. Apparently, Bo wasn't coming this year. The past hour, she had sat in this chair and waited on him. In all the years, he had never stood her up, but it appeared today he was a no-show. Slowly, she made her way to the counter and paid for her coffee.

Hurriedly, she trekked down the sidewalk and counted off the few blocks to the aged three-story apartment building she called home.

Funny, she couldn't remember what had drawn her to this old building that always needed upgrades. The entryway doors were aged and didn't even have peepholes in them. Small things like that she now realized were important.

Sam nervously looked around, then slipped her key in the lock and opened the door. Desperation rose in her throat and threatened to choke her. She needed to get a job so she could break free of the situation that threatened to consume her life.

Three months had passed since Tuttle Books sold to another bookstore and as a result several of the employees lost their jobs, hers included.

At first, she'd thought this was just a setback, but now the situation really caused her worry. Her money was dwindling away and any luxuries she may have wanted simply would wait.

Sam sat down on the side of her bed and took off her shoes. The fuzzy carpet tickled the bottom of her feet as she pulled on the loose strings with her toes.

For now, she was living on her savings and unemployment, something which made moving anywhere else impossible.

Sam's chest squeezed, her body tightened. She needed to find a job. She wondered what would happen if she didn't move and move quickly.

Staying here only added to the chance that she might get hurt.

Rob had turned into a nightmare with his constant badgering. His actions seemed to worsen with each day.

She stretched out in her bed as thoughts of the past couple months circled in her mind.

At first, Rob seemed to be a nice guy. They would talk when they passed each other in the hall or he'd start a conversation with her when they were both in the laundry room. After a while, she agreed to go out with him.

Sam tossed and pulled on her covers as she relived those times.

By their fifth date, she realized he was unstable. Oh, he seemed all right on the surface, but she soon learned he was a heavy drinker and alcohol brought out a dark, mean side of him.

She still cringed in remembrance of their last date. They went to Dante's Restaurant and unbeknownst to her, he'd started drinking beforehand. By the time the waiter brought the meal, he was becoming loud and belligerent.

The manager approached their table and told them to leave. That was the night she decided to end any pending relationship.

Standing there in front of the restaurant, she informed Rob she didn't want to go out with him anymore and to please not call her or ask her out again.

Since that night, he'd verbally taunted her and called her apartment at odd hours just to hang up. Of course, she couldn't prove the breather on the other end of the receiver was him. He made sure not to say anything over the phone, but in her heart she knew it was Rob.

Turning over, Sam shoved her hand under her pillow, determined to will her negative thoughts away.

Abruptly awoken, she jumped, sitting up with a jolt. The booming noise echoed through her apartment. It was drums beating — no, it was banging.

Turning her head, she blinked and tried to focus on the numbers on her clock that sat on her nightstand. What in the world was going on? It wasn't even seven o'clock in the morning.

The thumping increased rapidly. She pulled on her bedroom shoes while the commotion frantically persisted.

Reality struck and she swallowed hard. She knew who lurked behind the door. Even so, she would force herself to answer it. She didn't want the racket to wake Ms. West, the landlady. It was just too early in the morning and the old woman always blamed her for causing trouble. For some reason, she thought Sam encouraged Rob. Since he was her nephew, she refused to believe anything bad about him.

Forcing her feet to move, Sam willed herself to the entryway. She paused at the threshold then mustered the courage to open the door.

With a stiff back and a hard breath, Sam braced herself for what was to come. She cracked the door as far as the safety latched allowed.

Even through the small opening, she witnessed his cold rigid expression and knew nothing good lay behind those eyes.

Her only defense was to sound brave and stand firm.

Sam hesitated and forced down the familiar smothering sensation that filled her each time she confronted him. She had to be careful, like walking on eggs. She never knew what kind of ugly slurs he would spit or if he might try to force himself on her. Some of the remarks he threw...she definitely needed to keep her guard up. Sam feared the kinds of things he might be capable of.

Snarling, Rob gritted his teeth like an animal. He glared at Sam through bloodshot eyes from the drinking binge he had clearly been on. "Sam, let me in. We've played this game long enough. You need to realize...we belong together."

Sam shook her head and silently hoped he didn't hear the hammering of her heart. With forced bravery, she hid the weakness in her eyes.

She willed her emotions to stay in control. With a bold stance, she voiced her opinion to his statement of claim. "Rob, I told you there will never be anything between us. Just go away and leave me alone."

She reacted quickly before he put his hand or foot into the small opening and closed the door.

Rob slammed his fist against the hard wood, striking the door as he slurred out obscenities. The last words she heard were, "If I can't have you, no one will."

That final statement chilled her more than the wind outside.

She rubbed her goose-bumped arms and inhaled a deep breath as her quivering legs led her toward the kitchen.

Things were escalating. Sam remembered what the police said, which only made the situation worse. Did she want to hang around and *wait* to be hurt by this man?

No, she had to find a job. Then she would move out of this apartment and away from Rob as quickly as she could.

Back in her bedroom, Sam mentally calmed her shaking hands. She refused to let him get to her—somehow, she would find a way to end this. The answer to her problems was for her to find a job, that's all.

She paused putting on her lipstick and stared at the reflection that shined back at her from the mirror. Other than the occasional inner turmoil she faced, she didn't look too bad. Her hair could use a trim, but maybe she would let it grow for a while.

She was determined and optimistic that this would be the day she found employment. She quickly applied the final touch to her lips.

A scraping noise sounded in the hallway and her heart skipped.

She jumped and lipstick trailed its mark down her cheek.

Throwing down the tube, she spoke to her reflection. "Oh, what the heck! Look what I've done!" With a jittery hand, Sam harshly scrubbed at the pinkish line and wiped the smear off the side of her face.

All the while, she wondered how much longer she could take Rob's craziness. Over the weeks, his persistence had grown and he'd become harder to avoid.

After making certain no one was in the hallway, she quickly headed down the steps, determined to find employment.

Sam walked the city blocks and concentrated on checking out the job listings she circled in the newspaper.

As the day wore on, she watched the clouds move over the sun and noticed the gray in the sky.

Somehow, the changing weather seemed to make the day even drearier than she hoped. Pretty, clear skies always seem to put things in a better light.

Sam read her notes again and checked the addresses. With all her working experience in either retail or clerical, she felt certain she could find a job opening somewhere that would suit her.

Before crossing the street, she glanced at the front of a Mexican restaurant. A bittersweet memory flashed back to her. She remembered her days in high school and how she worked at a pizza place to make extra money. Cooking was not her first choice, but maybe she should check the local restaurants around town. Anything would work for now so she could move out of her place.

Hurrying to her appointments, Sam decided she would start thinking about food service.

The wind kicked up and whirled Sam's clothes. Grabbing her skirt, she rushed toward her last appointment. She hoped this interview would turn out better than the others.

Hours later, Sam unlocked the door to her apartment thinking about her last interview. Maybe the printing shop would call tomorrow. She did think the interview went exceptionally well and she certainly could answer phones and file.

As she tossed her jacket on the back of a chair, she glanced around her small living room. Even with the satisfaction of scheduling another interview, anxiety teetered, ready to choke her as if a hand slowly squeezing her throat.

Returning home should have been a retreat to peace, not a place where she didn't know from one minute to the next what would happen. It seemed her nerves jumped with every little sound.

Walking over to her small desk, she checked her messages. All she heard was the landlady's voice with a reminder that her rent was due.

A clap of thunder snapped her back to the present.

Her ears tuned to the raindrops that now pounded in a constant flow and a sigh of relief escaped her lips. At least she'd made it home before the rain began to fall.

Going into her kitchen, Sam pulled out a frozen pizza and smiled. For as long as she could remember, she liked pizza—even the store bought kind put a little zip in her spirit. A glimmer of hope sparked from somewhere deep within.

Putting her food in the oven to cook, Sam walked into the living room and turned on the television newscast. For some strange reason, the evening news seemed to lift her spirits. She supposed the newscast reminded her that everyone in the world faced problems and put hers in better perspective. At least she hadn't been shot or contracted some deadly disease.

Sam relaxed on her couch. Thinking back through the day, at least something productive happened. That put her in a better mood. Nothing would take away her newfound peace, not tonight anyway. The buzzing from the oven timer brought her attention back to the present and her meal that waited.

Taking a quick glance at the pizza pan on the table, she threw out a disgusted look. Mentally, she counted off the four slices she had eaten. With a shake of her head, she picked up the pizza pan, promising herself to take it to the kitchen later and half-heartedly dropping the round tin on the coffee table. Contented, she listened to a comedy on television while her eyes moved to the calendar that hung on the wall.

Tomorrow would be the third week of February. Somehow, deep in her heart the impression formed—this year her life would get better.

The last sound she heard as she drifted into a deep sleep was laughter coming from the portable box on her TV stand.

CHAPTER TWO

Sam's eyes popped open. She heaved a rapid breath.

A rough, sweaty hand rubbed her head. Hungry fingers clumsily caressed her hair and brushed against her cheek.

The air filled with an odd stench and assaulted her nose. Sam's stomach churned. She swallowed back the nausea that stirred from the pungent reek of liquor.

With a quick breath, she squelched the panic that bolted through her like lightening and concentrated on the eerie shadow that lurked above her head.

The light from a moonbeam shined across the room and created a spotlight on the staggering silhouette.

Immediately, she recognized Rob.

She jerked her body up in an instant.

Quickly, her head hit the couch hard as her body slammed down tight with the cushions. Rob lashed out and grabbed the front of her blouse. The gold-colored shiny circles popped off as the cotton material ripped.

Sam clawed his face, managing to pull away and scramble to her feet.

She forged the strength from somewhere deep within and gave him a quick shove. His body fell backward.

Her heart leapt as she raced toward the simmering glow coming from the nightlight in the hallway. Rob dashed after her like a dog snapping at her heels.

As Sam approached her front door, her peripheral vision glimpsed the statue made of metal perched on the shelf over her coat rack. She knew the little figurine wouldn't offer much defense because it was small and hollow, but what other choice did she have?

Quickly, she snatched up the horse. She whacked Rob, hitting him hard, then another time, until he staggered and fell.

Sam ran as fast as she could and left Rob lying on the hallway floor. A moan escaped his lips as a trickle of blood oozed from his head.

She scurried down the steps as remorse hit her. Of all the stupid things she could've done! Why had she forgotten to lock her door?

Sam dashed down the sidewalk. She was aware, vaguely, of the passing city blocks.

The sting of the air in her eyes, on her cheeks, slowly revealed the brutal chill. The February night embraced her entire body. Her skin tingled as the wintry air swirled inside her torn garment.

With shivering hands, Sam grabbed the fabric and held tight. She blinked and fought against tears as they trickled down her cheek. This was no time to cry—she needed to stay strong.

Blurred with emotion, she was grateful for living in the city. The streetlights shined on the sidewalk and gave her a clear path in the night.

After a few blocks, she slowed down to a jog, finally able to stop running. Sam's heart beat in rapid succession as she leaned against a building and heaved, barely aware of the frosty concrete pressed against her back.

Sam concentrated on inhaling slow breaths in and out, until her lungs felt normal again.

She slid down the rough surface and landed flat on the icy sidewalk. Crouched down, Sam held her ribs as they throbbed.

Rubbing her cheeks, she swiped away the moisture that flowed over her face.

No, she wouldn't give in to despair. Now she could go back to the police and get help. Maybe, with a court order, she could keep Rob away. She could concentrate on getting her life back on the right track.

Sam sat there in the dismal hour of darkness and focused on calming her shaky nerves.

Her emotions drained her. Hunkered down on the sidewalk mindlessly, Sam watched the nightlife across the street.

After what seemed like hours, pins and needles pricked her frigid, stiff body. She clutched at her torn top and shivered once more. How could she have nowhere to go? How did she manage to lose connections to all her friends? They had all married or moved away.

Totally alone, she knew there was no other choice but to return home.

Sam cautiously climbed the steps to the hallway of her apartment door.

She searched and found no Rob in sight. Relieved, her body relaxed as she released the air she held in her lungs. Sam slammed the door and bolted the lock, then rushed into her bedroom. Violently she threw the ripped top to the floor before falling across her bed like a limp rag.

Now she was sure Rob could be dangerous. Maybe this time when she went to the police, they would listen.

Tomorrow, she would go see that officer she spoke with and demand a restraining order.

As the tears began once again to roll down the sides of her face, she fantasized about moving. Mentally, she added up her savings and contemplated ways to accumulate the extra money for the deposit on a different apartment. Even though she loved living in the city, her meager unemployment didn't even cover all the rent on her little place.

The next day, Sam sat at her kitchen table and sipped her coffee. She had gathered up the energy for a hot shower to relieve the soreness in her body and now sat bundled in a warm, terrycloth robe.

A knock intruded on her solitude. She jumped at the sound and her hand went to her side.

Sam's spine stiffened. The events of the night before flashed in her mind.

No, please not Rob again. She was so tired of this situation. Forging a strong determination to end his harassment for the last time, she rose and rigidly walked toward the door. "Rob, you leave me alone! I have had enough of you. This is going to stop today."

A baritone voice she didn't recognize loudly eased through the wood. "Ms. Samantha Blacker?"

Sam leaned in close to the door curiously. "Yes, who is there?"

A man cleared his throat. "My name is Clarence Wright. I'm an attorney at Wright and Boyd."

With a huff, Sam braced herself for whatever faced her on the other side of the entryway. She couldn't help but suspect the lawyer had something to do with Rob.

Unlocking her door, she searched the man's face and started quickly to speak. "I'm glad you're here. The guy barged into my house in the middle of the night and—"

The short stocky man watched Sam with an expression of impatience and interrupted her. Normally, he wouldn't have contacted someone this way, but he needed to be in this part of the city anyway, so by fate he stood at her doorway.

"Excuse me, Miss. You are Samantha Blacker, right?"

The intended words Sam planned to say faded as she shook her head in agreement.

The man smiled and handed her his business card. "Good. I need you to come down to my office. There's a will that needs to be settled and you're named as the beneficiary."

Sam's brow wrinkled as she reached for the card. "What will are you talking about?"

The lawyer's eyes showed sincerity as he scanned her face. "Ms. Blacker, I'm sorry that I have to tell you this, but John Bolden Winston has passed away."

Sam felt relieved after hearing the stranger's name. She knew then that she wasn't the woman he was searching for. "I am sorry, Mr. Wright. I don't know any John Winston. Please, I have a lot to do today."

She started to shut the door but Mr. Wright placed his hand on the side of the frame. "Ms. Blacker, please. I'm looking for Samantha Blacker. She works at Tuttle Books and drives a yellow Volkswagen."

She stopped quickly, her hand gripping the knob.

Sam stared at the short man, unsure if she wanted to make a comment. Finally, in a voice almost inaudible, she answered, "Yes, well that is my car, and I did work at Tuttle's about a year ago."

Mr. Wright flashed his confident smile. "Then you are the Samantha Blacker I was searching for. You can review the office hours on my card. Call my secretary and set up an appointment so we can discuss everything."

He nodded his head and began to walk away. Hesitating, he paused and added, "Just don't wait too long, Ms. Blacker. This is important. We need to settle this matter as soon as possible."

Sam shut the door. Her fingers slid over the raised letters on the card then she tossed the thin cardboard on her coffee table.

How odd. She wondered how she got herself into these situations. John Winston was a stranger—definitely not family, nor a friend she could recall.

A few hours later, Sam walked into the brisk morning air. The sun shined as if it promised new beginnings. That gave her hope for a good day to come, a day full of possibilities.

By that afternoon Sam's legs felt like cement as she dragged them up her apartment steps. The ordeal of the night before and her morning at the police station had left her emotionally zapped. The only thing she wanted to do was curl up on the couch with a cup of hot chocolate.

Inside, she moved to the small desk and punched on her answering machine. With a shake of her head, she listened to the buzzing sound of no messages.

Sam's hopes popped like a balloon. She really believed she would get a call from one of those interviews she attended yesterday morning.

She had the job experience and could perform the jobs. Why didn't she receive a call back?

Later that evening Sam put her bowl, now empty of the soup she had eaten, in the kitchen sink. She ambled back into the living room and sat down on the couch, lost in thoughts of the past.

The television blared out a commercial about a cowboy movie. Seeing it brought to mind Bo talking about enjoying old movies. Sam repeated something he would say to her on occasion. "Have faith and everything works out in due time."

Her mind's eye watched Bo as he got into his car the last day she saw him. She wondered where he was tonight and why she didn't get to talk with him this year.

Sam recollected a particular conversation with Bo. One of the many where he always talked about the Lord. At first, listening to him recite things from the Bible made her uncomfortable. Soon though she realized that was just his way. He always quoted a scripture if he believed it would offer comfort.

Sam stretched out and flinched because of her still achy side.

She'd owned up to the fact that Bo was a different kind of friend. She never knew anyone in her life who believed in God the way he did. When they talked, often times he would say something religious to her.

Sam smiled to herself as she unconsciously picked at a piece of lint that lay on the side of her sofa. At least Bo never said anything negative to her. He would just suggest things and of course, he talked about Jesus.

After all these years, she now expected him to bring up some scripture of the gospel. A lot of the time, she was curious to see what he would say.

A feeling of warmth floated through her. The uncle she never had—that's what she pretended he was to her. He certainly understood how to give her peace and contentment about matters that otherwise tormented her.

That was why she wanted to talk to him about Rob. After all, there was only so much the police could do.

Her mind continued to stroll through her life. She recalled her mom, who died in a car wreck. That had been so many years ago. Never knowing her father, her grandmother stepped to rear her.

Sadness washed over Sam. How she missed Grandma. Times like these were when she summoned up some of the talks they used to have. That special way she had of viewing situations that made everyone Grandma knew see things differently.

Sam just couldn't understand it. Why did God take loved ones away, especially from someone so young? What good could possibly come from a child losing the only family she had? Oh, she had listened to Bo and his explanations, but still it made no sense to her.

Sam harked back to that hot August day soon after she graduated. She came home to find their house on fire. They rushed her grandmother to the hospital, but her lungs couldn't handle the smoke she inhaled.

Staring at the ceiling, Sam mulled over things. The one good thing in her life now was her friend Bo. But when she needed him so much, he'd missed their last meeting.

Sam made a silent vow. She'd attend the convention herself next year if she had to, but when she saw him next, she was going to pay more attention to what he said and exchange phone numbers with him.

She relaxed as she started to recall some of the things he said to her. His words of comfort lulled her into a soothing sleep.

Waking up the next morning, Sam felt the warmth from the sun peek through the curtain. She stretched and cast her eyes over her living room. She'd fallen asleep on the couch again. Sitting up, she rubbed the back of her neck and massaged the stiffness out.

Her eyes followed the beam of sunlight from across the room. The glow spotlighted Mr. Wright's business card and highlighted his office number.

Sam picked up the card, fingering the letters. Why did that lawyer think she was the woman he was looking for?

On impulse, she wandered over to the small table that held her phone.

Five minutes later, Sam placed the receiver back in the cradle. A two o'clock appointment had been available.

In the kitchen, she bathed in the quiet of the morning. So far, her day was getting off to a good start. Since she was going across town to the lawyer's office, she would see what businesses were on that block. Maybe she could find a job in that section of the city.

She carried her cup of coffee with her to the bedroom and prepared for her day.

Recalling something Bo said to her a while back perked her up and gave her the inspiration she needed to head out and find that job.

CHAPTER THREE

Reviewing the streets, she spotted a woman with kids. Another woman wiped a smudge off a little girl's face.

Melancholy washed through her as she examined her life. She pondered why she wasn't married and raising kids. Sam watched as a little boy pulled his mother's hand while he rushed to the hotdog vendor.

She wishfully wondered when the God that Bo always spoke of would smile down on her life. But it seemed He never did.

Strolling through the edge of the park, she studied the busy street traffic. Sam did enjoy living in the city. She couldn't imagine being anywhere else. She just needed to move to the north side of Atlanta, away from Rob.

Sam thought about areas with apartments in them. She planned to stay within walking distance of the bus stops. That saved the mileage from adding up on her old VW.

She paused as she remembered the purchase of her vehicle. It was part of the small settlement from her grandmother's insurance. Such a long time ago, she thought.

A jogger pounded down a winding path through the park. Further down, someone walked his dog.

With a contented breath, Sam picked up her pace.

Yes, she was very happy to live in the city where everything was so convenient.

Crossing the street, Sam arrived at a modern white brick building. According to the address on the business card, this was where the office of Wright and Boyd was located.

Inside the entrance, she walked toward the elevator. Sam glanced down at the marble floor at the shine that cast a shadow as her feet made their way inside the steel doors.

Pressing the button to the fifth floor, she fidgeted with her clothes and second-guessed herself. Of course she wasn't the woman Mr. Wright wanted to find. Why was she wasting her time?

Sam left the elevator and came to the open waiting area. Her eyes landed on a gray-haired receptionist sitting at a big glass desk.

The older woman raised her head and glared over her glasses toward Sam, speaking impatiently. "Yes, can I help you?"

Something about the demeanor of the woman made Sam hesitate before she answered.

Silently, she decided she came this far, so she would just get this appointment over with. "I am here to see Mr. Wright. My name is Samantha Blacker."

Reading her appointment book, the older woman quickly pointed her finger toward a chair. "Yes well, have a seat. He'll be back from lunch anytime."

Sam picked up a magazine with last year's date—anything to keep her mind busy. Even a story about the effects of global warming should distract her for a few minutes.

On the third page of the article, Mr. Wright stepped off the elevator.

He picked up his stack of mail off the receptionist's desk and spotted Sam. "Good afternoon, Ms. Blacker. Come into my office."

Sam stood and smoothed down her pants, uncomfortable with the smug tone of his voice.

"Mr. Wright, I know this is a misunderstanding. I just came so you can mark me off your list and find the right woman."

The stocky man paid no attention to what Sam said. He led her to his door and motioned for her to go inside.

Settled on the edge of a large leather chair, Sam shivered as coolness from the material sent a chill through her slacks. She curiously watched Mr. Wright as he skimmed through the papers in a file folder.

"Mr. Wright, I really am at a loss about what to say, but I'm sure I don't know a Mr. Winston. I can't figure out how you concluded that I am the lady you are searching for. Surely, you must have your facts wrong."

As he pulled out a letter from his files, he shot an aggravated look Sam's way. "Ms. Blacker, if we can just go over a few things then we will clear this up."

As Mr. Wright studied the letter, he addressed Sam in a matter-of-fact way. "You live at two-hundred Pine Place, Atlanta, Georgia. You work, or used to work, at Tuttle Books and presently you drive a nineteen-ninety-seven yellow Volkswagen."

Sam crinkled her face at the sound his voice made when he remarked about her car. Defensively she said, "Yes, but I don't understand what that has to do with any of this."

Mr. Wright rearranged the papers and leaned back in his chair. His eyes narrowed as he observed Sam.

"No, I understand you don't. I must admit this is an odd situation. I don't believe I have ever encountered a will like this before, but it seemed that John Winston didn't have a lot of up-to-date information about Samantha Blacker. He included a letter in the will that goes over what he knew."

The well-dressed man pulled his chair closer to his desk and flipped pages.

"Mr. Winston came to Georgia once a year for a restaurant convention. Apparently, he and Ms. Blacker would meet at Baker's Sandwich Shop. He wrote that he has known her for five years. She worked at Tuttle Books and drove a yellow VW."

Mr. Wright turned the letter over as he continued. "The man also stated that her grandmother raised her from around the age of twelve. Ms. Blacker, John Winston spoke of you as the daughter he never had and requested in his will that I try to persuade you to keep his business running."

Sam breathed in quickly. Her heart beat in rapid successions as she sat there still as stone.

Total foreboding closed in around her. Shock soaked through her like a sponge. The words he said bounced around in her ears.

Inching forward, she perched herself on the edge of the chair. All she wanted to do now was leave his office and pretend she didn't know the lawyer was talking about Bo.

Sam felt queasy and slid her hands down her face. The more she heard, the more she suspected John Bolden Winston was her friend Bo.

Her head started to spin. She clasped her now clammy hands together and twisted them nervously.

She really wished she could believe this person was someone else. Gulping for air, she spoke with caution as she repeated some things he said. "I did know Bo—John—he was my friend," she acknowledged. "He never told me his real name."

The lawyer rose from his swivel chair and walked past Sam toward the water pitcher.

He watched her face turn the color of paste and hoped she wouldn't pass out. He always hated this part of his job. Handing her a glass of water, he listened as Sam started to speak.

"I think Bo was always trying to make me see I needed to believe in God. He talked about the Lord a lot. He had a strong faith."

Standing, she went across the room and faced the window. "I wish I had been able to spend more time with him."

Turning to face Mr. Wright, she asked, "What happened to Bo?"

Mr. Wright eyed Sam as she sat back down in the chair. Then he pulled out a different envelope. "John Winston had a bad case of pneumonia. He was in the hospital a week before he died."

Watching Sam intently, he continued. "Apparently, he made up his will a couple of days before. You probably know that Mr. Winston lost his wife ten years ago and they never had any children. He left what he owned to you."

Confused, Sam turned to face him. Lines creased around her mouth. "To me? Are you sure?"

Hesitating, Mr. Wright replied, "Yes, Ms. Blacker. He left his estate to you and in all rights, everything is yours, or could be anyway."

Sam turned her head to the man tapping an envelope and gave him a questioning look. "What do you mean 'could be'?"

Mr. Wright took a sip of water from the glass that sat on his desk and proceeded to read from his file. "The property consists of twenty acres of land located in the small rural town of Big Fork Lake, Alabama, including an inn with ten small cabins, which he rented to tourists.

"He called the place Big Fork Inn & Eats. Mr. Winston's living quarters were in the two-bedroom apartment located over the business."

Sam sat in the chair bewildered and her mind drifted to memories of Bo. She stared at her hands, only half-aware as Mr. Wright explained.

"There are certain specifications attached to the will." Mr. Wright stopped for a second and eyed Sam in an attempt to get her full attention. "Ms. Blacker, are you listening?"

Shaking away her thoughts, Sam snapped back to the conversation and wobbled her head. "Yes, Mr. Wright, I am listening."

He closed the file and folded his hands together on the desk.

"Ms. Blacker, his will states that you have to live there for a year. After a year, the inn becomes yours. If within that year you leave or decide you don't want the property, it would go to the Town of Big Fork Lake, Alabama.

"Furthermore, you only have thirty days from today to decide or you forfeit everything."

Mr. Wright stood and handed Sam a sealed envelope with her name scribbled on the front. "He left this letter for you."

Sam rose from her seat and drew a hard breath as she reached out to grasp hold of the paper. She turned and headed toward his office door to leave. "Thanks, Mr. Wright. I'll be in touch."

The short man spoke rapidly before she closed the door. "Ms. Blacker, I have the keys and the directions if and when you're ready. Think this over and give me a call, but remember—thirty days."

Sam walked out of the office and forced her stiff legs to carry her. Concentrating on the elevator, she moved past the receptionist out of the building as fast as possible.

True, she didn't know a lot about Bo's personal life, but they were friends. He had been her best friend of late.

When they did talk, she shared some of her private feelings with him. She told many things to Bo. She could trust him.

Sam walked aimlessly. At that moment, her life had changed.

She would miss her talks with him. Even his being a Christian hadn't made any difference. He was a good man. It was his business if he had trusted in God. Still, she was amazed that he accepted things the way he did. He acted as if everybody had to deal with the same stuff. Inwardly, Sam believed that God had his favorites and she hadn't been one of them. Not even when she was little.

The wind picked up and Sam barely noticed the change. She strolled as the words Mr. Wright said played in her mind.

An inn and an apartment in a little rural town, somewhere in Alabama...what would she do?

True, she needed a change. But to move to a small backwoods place in the sticks was certainly not her first choice.

Briefly, Sam scanned the streets. Why would she want to leave the comfort of the city? It offered everything she needed. To be shut off from the world in some rural area scared her. She clutched her hand and swallowed hard at the thought. The busy streets, the hustle of people that at least made her feel as if she had a purpose, even if she hadn't figured out what it was yet.

Sam hurried down the path in a fog and headed to the park entrance.

Her heart ached as she tried to accept what the lawyer said. There was no mistake. Her friend Bo was gone. Forever.

First, she let her friends slip away. Now, she'd lost Bo.

Why did he have to go?

Sam spotted a bench. She dropped down on the hard, splintery surface and paid no attention to the fact that part of the wood was broken off.

She rested motionless, deadened to anything going on around her. Her mind traveled back to her last conversation with Bo and searched for clues as to what to do now.

Sam wiped a spot off her purse, remembering Bo asked her to open her heart and try the Lord. Bo was different. He believed that all people had some good in them. What would it be like to live every day trusting in God to lead you? She closed her eyes momentarily and shook her head, mumbling, "Yeah right Sam, as if that would help anything." Straightening, she suddenly focused on her surroundings. Her eyes shifted to her watch and she noticed that an hour had already passed.

The clouds had grown darker and Sam lifted her head toward the sky. She grunted. At least now the weather matched her mood.

Her coat started to show spots of water and forced her to rise and hurry home.

Inside the door of her tiny apartment, Sam shook the water off her jacket and hung it to dry.

The next couple of hours ticked by slowly as Sam busied herself with her cleaning, still disoriented from learning about Bo.

She obediently made herself open the mail and tossed all the junk letters in the kitchen trash.

Walking past her computer, Sam paused. What kind of information would she find out about that town? Would there be any important stuff to know about such a small dot on the map?

Sam watched the scenes on the monitor as she steered her mouse to the different links.

She surfed from one site to another and studied the pictures that showed different holiday exhibitions and events of Big Fork Lake, Alabama. It looked like a decent place, pretty, but small. One of those towns where everyone knew your name and your business, whether you wanted them to or not. What was she going to do?

She told herself if she could stand Nowheresville for a year, the town would pay her to take the inn. That way, she'd have money to move somewhere decent and they could have their inn.

Searching online did provide Sam with many pictures. The main attraction appeared to be the lake. There were lots of facts about fishing in the area. She found numerous stories and candid photos of some local events.

After an hour, Sam flipped off the switch and gazed at the black screen.

She didn't know what to do. She admitted the pictures made Big Fork Lake, Alabama seem nice. Victorian style houses and large oak trees surrounded the town that sported a beautiful lake stretched alongside its outskirts.

That still didn't change the fact that Big Fork Lake was only a little tourist town with Mom and Pop stores scattered about. She didn't see many things going on within its city limits. Heck, she couldn't even find a listing for a nearby Wal-Mart.

Even if she did stay at home a lot, it was still nice to live somewhere that offered things such as entertainment if she decided she needed a night out. She was lacking friends already, but at least the comfort of chatter and people surrounded her daily. If she didn't want to feel alone, all she had to do was walk out her apartment door.

A smile escaped her lips as she thought of the little girl she was used to chitchatting with. It'd become a weekly habit to stop by the bagel shop. Nora, the owner, always had her daughter Tabitha with her on Wednesday evenings. As soon a Sam walked in the door and ordered, the child ran over to her table to show her the latest drawings she had done in preschool.

She also enjoyed the chats she had with the young couple who waited at the bus stop every morning. She had never asked their names, but knew they were married and worked at the same business by some of the things they'd said.

The prospect of starting over in a place so secluded overwhelmed her.

The sound of a thunderous knock drew her attention and her body jumped as she was pulled back to her present troubles. Her stomach did a flip-flop as her mind leapt to Rob.

The beating continued echoing through her small apartment.

During the noise, she heard an old wiry voice screech, "Samantha, I know you're home. I saw you come in. You open this door!"

Sam gasped with relief as she recognized the voice of old Ms. West, her property owner. Scooting out of her chair, she headed to the door. On the way, she remembered the rent. She'd been so consumed with trying to find a job, she forgot to draw the rent money out of her savings account.

Sam didn't have enough money in her checking account to write a check to cover the rent. She chose to keep most of her money in savings. That made it easier for her to control spending.

Straightening her t-shirt, Sam opened the door and faced the spunky little woman.

The picture of Ms. West's frail body as the little woman stood there with an expression of wrath made her smile.

"Yes, Ms. West, can I help you?"

Ms. West glared at Sam with a scolding expression. "You know your rent is due, young lady. Two weeks have gone by and I need my money."

Leaning against the door, Sam nodded her head. "Ms. West, I am sorry. I have been job hunting and I completely forgot about the rent."

The old woman stood there in her plaid housecoat and slippers, narrowing her eyes at Sam. "Well, if you don't want to search for a new place to live as well, I need the money. Now!"

Closing her eyes for a second, Sam tried to calm down the situation. "Yes, Ms. West, I do apologize. I will get your money out of the bank tomorrow first thing and be over to pay you."

Ms. West frowned at Sam over her glasses with disbelief. After a few seconds, her hoarse voice rang out. "Fine, but I need that rent by tomorrow at five." Squinting her face, she examined Sam closely. "Or you're out!"

Finally, the older woman turned and started to slowly make her way toward the end of the hall.

Sam shut the door and shook her head as she listened to the drip of raindrops on the window. The sound of banging on the door once again jolted her from the tranquil moment.

Sam rubbed her temple. If only Ms. West could be happy with tomorrow's date.

But Ms. West was relentless and no doubt had returned to ask her to write a check out. She hated having to explain things to the old woman.

Hastily, she moved back to the door and opened it prepared with an explanation as to why she could not give her a check. Sam formed the words on her lips and started to speak when she encountered a snarling look of satisfaction.

Rob tried to shove the door the rest of the way open, but alcohol weakened his strength.

Staggering, he slurred his words at Sam. "Yea, nnnow I havvvve you."

Reaching for her, he grabbed air as Sam quickly moved back. "I've taken out a restraining order!" she warned. "You should have been served by now. Stay away!"

Cussing, Rob balled up his fist and aimed for Sam's face.

She moved fast and jerked back as she yelled.

Quickly she stepped forward, gave his body a shove and slammed the door.

Rushing, she latched both locks as fast as she could.

Sam leaned against the door with her eyes closed in thanks as she listened to the clumsy ruckus as he staggered to his feet.

The next thing Sam heard was Ms. West's hurried footsteps march down the hall.

She turned her ear, listening to the muffled sounds. Sam couldn't understand everything that was said, but by the stern tone of woman's voice, she guessed Rob was being reprimanded.

Then the stomping started as Rob bounded down the steps to escape the older woman's wrath.

Sam rubbed her chin as she walked toward the bedroom. She knew Ms. West loved her nephew, but she only hoped that one day the older lady would see he had a problem and talk him into getting help.

Nevertheless, she couldn't help but worry what might have happened if Rob was not completely wasted when he attacked her. She marched to the phone to call the police, but hesitated, considering acting on the restraining order and realizing she better not. She might get Rob temporarily off her back, but Ms. West would kick her out. Her being behind on rent would only give the lady justification.

Suddenly, her perspective cleared. Sam accepted what she knew in her heart. This whole situation with Rob was crazy and she had no other choice.

She wanted to get out of this predicament—whether she liked the place or not wasn't the issue right now. Bo gave her a new life or at least a chance for one. All she needed to do was reach out and grab hold.

Maybe the place was a hick town in the boonies. But what other choice did she have? Besides, she could live there for a year. She could do anything for a mere year.

Remembering what Mr. Wright said, Sam drew a hard breath. Either a year in Big Fork Lake or another day in frantic search for a job so she could move.

Sam walked back to the living room with a determined stance. She made her decision. She was going to get away from Rob.

CHAPTER FOUR

Sam paid no attention to the time as she dialed the number. On the fourth ring, Mr. Wright picked up the phone.

Ten minutes later, Sam hung her phone up. Her mind reeled with plans to leave as soon as possible. She went over the things she needed to do to make a fast get away early the next morning.

Sam mentally listed all the places she needed to visit. She decided to stop by the bank and close out her accounts before she went to Mr. Wright's office to pick up the keys and driving directions to Big Fork Lake, Alabama.

She teetered between apprehension and excitement. Taking her clothes from the closet, she tossed them on the bed. Every so often, she would stop and contemplate things.

Sam wasn't sure where she was going or what she would find when she arrived there. What was the town of Big Fork Lake, Alabama going to be like?

After she sorted her clothes, she picked up her purse and headed out the door on a mission.

Sam remembered there was a twenty-four-hour Quick Mart a mile down the road. As she grabbed her car keys and purse, she hoped she could get some empty boxes to pack in.

Her feet floated down the steps as she headed toward the opening of the apartment building into the night.

Stopping instantly, Sam froze in her spot. She backed up tight against the brick wall. Motionless, she hid in the dark.

Silently, Sam watched across the street. There, in the shadow of the night under the streetlight, she witnessed Rob hop into an old, dark color pick-up truck and speed off down the road.

A sigh of relief escaped her lips.

She didn't remember him driving a truck. Last she saw, he owned a sedan, but who cared anyway? At least he was gone for now. All she wanted was to leave without any trouble.

Over the next few hours, she packed her clothes, dishes, sheets and towels. Next, Sam concentrated on cleaning. Then finally, she trekked back and forth to her car hauling her personal items to take with her.

As Sam cleared off her dresser, she put an old music box she'd hung on to since she was a small girl in the last box she was packing.

Her sight floated to the letter Mr. Wright gave her.

Apprehensions tightened around her. She couldn't understand why she felt anxious about reading the letter, but she just couldn't bring herself to do so yet. Sam carried the long envelope to the table by the door and laid it beside her purse.

Surveying the apartment, she took one last tour of her surroundings to make sure she'd packed all the things she wanted.

Stopping in front of her kitchen window, she watched the cars go down street. With remorse, she stared one last time at the street below and the busy nightlife in Atlanta.

Inwardly, Sam promised herself that this would be a clean start. No matter what this small town was like, one way or another, she would use this year to get her life back on the right track.

The next morning, before the sun had risen, Sam jolted awake. Old habits had her listening for any odd noises.

She was relieved that the last thing she remembered doing before she crashed on the couch was to double check her locks on the door, sometime after two.

Sam grabbed the clothes she laid out the night before and smiled—time to face the unknown.

With a fast shower behind her, she dressed in her comfortable jeans and a sweatshirt for the long drive. Before she dashed out the door she scribbled a note for Ms. West promising to give her a call.

As Sam sat in her car, she shifted the boxes, wondering how she managed to jam all of them in her car. Thank goodness she was able to pack everything she wanted. The only place left empty was a very a small spot on the passenger's seat just big enough for her purse.

Sam turned her little car around and headed the few blocks toward the bank. Since this would be her last meal in her hometown, she headed to her favorite coffee shop.

A short while later, Sam perched on the seat sipping her coffee. Taking in her surroundings, she counted down the time until the bank and offices opened. Staring out the window of the café, mixed emotions tugged at her, excitement and sadness all jumbled together. Even though she didn't want to leave, an eagerness for a change to her situation had her anticipating what lie ahead. What is it really like in a small town?

She couldn't remember living anywhere else but here. When she was small, she and her mother lived eight miles out of town, but the area was still considered Atlanta and close to amenities.

At nine-forty, Sam stepped out of Mr. Wright's office.

She stood beside her VW. She'd already called Ms. West and left her a message that something had come up and she had to leave town. She assured her that a money order for the rent was in the mail and asked her to dispose of anything in the apartment the older woman didn't want.

All the papers from the lawyer's office were signed and she was holding the keys to her home and apparently, her new business. A fresh life stared back at her.

With her hand wrapped tight around the keys, she smiled. Anyway, she had a chance for a start somewhere else. She would take the year in Alabama and map out where she really wanted to live. With the sale of the place next year, she could live just about anywhere she chose. Maybe a popular beach in Florida. Or New York City.

Driving toward the interstate, Sam spotted an all too familiar road.

Sudden heaviness weighed at her heart and she slowed down as sadness blanketed her. This was the final block before she made her exit to freedom.

Taking a right, Sam pulled between the iron gates into the entrance of Grace Memorial Rest.

After parking, Sam walked to her grandmother's grave and tugged her coat around her. The air stabbed her, causing a shiver. As she bent down to the headstone, heartbreak assaulted her the way it always did.

Shaking her head, she tried to ignore the stab of guilt, knowing she failed to visit as much as she should have. On the other side of the grave, she looked to the familiar spot where her mother lay at rest, both of them side-by-side just as her grandmother requested.

Sam swallowed hard. Even after all these years, she still fought to keep from crying. In her heart, she felt as if time stood still, the loss still fresh.

Tears stung the back of her eyes. Biting her lip, she rubbed the cold, jagged headstones. This was her goodbye, at least for a while.

Sam mumbled a few words of love as she continued to caress the rough stone with her mother's name carved on the front.

Straightening, she walked around to the other side of the grave. Although she loved her mother, her grandmother was the one who held most of her heart.

She couldn't stop the need to say what she felt even if she wanted to. "I'm going to move, Grandma." Sam wrung her hands as she glanced from one headstone to another. "I have to get out of this town."

She paused and listened to the sounds of construction work somewhere in the distance. Her attention shifted back to the headstones. She focused on her grandmother's as she continued to speak. "I have a chance for a new start—things in my life have gotten out of hand."

She paused as her eyes searched both graves. Then one last time she spoke to the headstones. "No matter where I go to, both of you will always be with me in my heart."

Seated in her car, Sam stared one last time at the spaces that held pieces of her love. She tried to memorize the shapes and scenery that outlined the special section.

Then slowly, she drove down the narrow curvy drive past the entrance of Grace Memorial Rest.

The radio blared as she drove the miles away. The once heavy traffic cleared and made her four-hour drive toward Alabama easier.

Sam's sight focused on the seat where the letter Bo had written gawked back at her.

Hurriedly, she looked away, still uneasy about reading the words. Bo had never been anything but kind to her. He was just a plain, down-to-earth guy. Sometimes he would speak his mind about a situation if it went against his beliefs. Always though, he would talk about his faith and often mentioned how Jesus helped him.

Whatever was in the letter, it would be something to encourage her. At least, she hoped.

She stepped down on the gas pedal and glanced around. It had been a long time since she went on a trip. Her last driving vacation had been three years ago when she traveled to the coast for a week.

That was one thing she liked about living in the city. The busses made it easy to get around without having to put miles on your car.

Before Sam realized, two hours of cruising on the open road passed and another long hour crept by crawling down the interstate at an irritatingly slow speed because of an accident. In an attempt to get comfortable, she awkwardly tried to stretch out her legs and at the same time massaged her neck. Sam really had forgotten how tired driving a long distance made someone.

She gazed at the scenery. Still, despite her stiff, aching body from sitting still, she realized she did enjoy driving. Somehow it relaxed her to see new sights. Homes and yards of all shapes and sizes. Maybe, when this year ended, she would find somewhere to live close to a city for the easy commute, but that still offered her a small yard. Somewhere she could plant a flower or two. Wherever that would be.

Thirty minutes later, a rest stop came in view and Sam turned on to the exit and pulled in. She turned off her engine and rubbed her eyes as they automatically fell on the letter.

She took her one last excuse to head to the restroom and grab a soda from the nearby vending machine to delay the inevitable.

With her legs now limber after the long drive, she ambled back to her Volkswagen and settled in her car.

Sam popped the top on her soda and focused on the letter. Her hands trembled with anticipation as she picked up the white envelope.

The handwriting on the front somehow made her feel close to Bo. Cautiously, she unfolded the page and concentrated on the words written by a dying man.

Dearest Sam,

By now, you are aware that I am gone. There is no need to cry for me. I just wanted you to know you have been a good friend.

I realize we only saw each other once a year, but I enjoyed your company very much.

It's time now, Sam, for me to go be with the Lord and see my sweet Elaine again. We will be together forever more and I sure have missed her.

You, my dear Sam, need a stable home and a life with the Lord. I have given you the home. Just try it for a year.

If you don't like Big Fork Lake, you have my blessings to move on.

As for the Lord, Sam, you know what I have always tried to tell you. He is with you no matter where you go. You just have to give him a chance and open your heart.

The inn has guests who come every year and town folk that stop by for sandwiches and desserts. It's nothing fancy, but it has kept me going and been a part of my life for as long as I care to remember.

My home is yours now, to do with as you please after the first year. It's my hope that within this year you will find that you like Big Fork Lake and make it your home.

You will meet the girls who work there and my friend Noah.

Anne Doyle is older like me. She is a bit snappy at times, but I've never believed she means to be.

Belle McBride hasn't been out of high school but a few years. She's a hardworking girl who has found the inner peace we all need at times.

Then there's Noah Frye. I have known him all his life and he is like a son to me. I like to think that maybe I have helped him to become the fine man he is. I hope you two can become friends.

Sam, trust the Lord, and things will work out.

Love to you my friend,

Bo Winston

Sam folded the letter and stared at the front of the envelope. Her watery eyes blurred.

Unhurriedly, she guided her shaky hands to the glove compartment. Ever so carefully, she tucked the letter inside for safekeeping.

Sam's lips quivered as she succumbed to the pain of raw hurt. Resting her head on the back of the seat, tears tinkled down her cheeks and Sam's body shook as she gave in to the anguish. How could God take someone so kind? She cried for herself and for Bo.

She continued to sob for her grandmother and mother and for life gone wrong.

When she could weep no more, Sam sat there mentally drenched. She closed her eyes and steadied her breath as calmness slowly covered her.

Some while later, she opened her eyes and cursed because she fell asleep in her car. A glance to her watch revealed hours had past. She lifted her head and remembered the letter, now more determined than ever to find some of the peace Bo had boasted in his life.

Headed back down I-165 toward Big Fork Lake, Alabama, Sam finally passed through Montgomery and turned off the exit to her destination.

She braked at the only stop light in Big Fork Lake. Using the glow from a nearby street light, Sam glanced down at her watch and gauged the time.

Almost nine. She was drained and her body stiff. All she wanted was somewhere to lie down.

She forced herself to pay extra attention to the road signs. Mr. Wright said the area seemed to be easy to find. She agreed with him. The city limits were only a few miles from the exit.

She only wished it weren't dark so she could see what the place really looked like.

Sam thought back to the pictures she'd seen on the computer. She would have enjoyed arriving in the daylight.

After driving two miles out of town, she smiled at the few houses that stood scattered along the road, yellow beams shining through and lighting the interiors. Sam admired the big windows in the older Victorian houses. Even the smaller homes held a fascinating charm all their own.

She peered down a side street and could just barely see the reflection of a small apartment complex on her left.

As Sam turned right on the road that led her to the inn, she marveled at the area. What a difference this place was from Atlanta, Georgia.

A white picket fence came into view and Sam's headlights illuminated the enclosure. She noticed then that the trellis surrounded a big open parking lot. There, she spotted the drive that wound into the inn.

She blinked as she pulled into the parking lot, trying to clear away some of her tiredness and adjust her eyes. She hadn't expected how black everything would seem in the country. She was used to all the city lights.

The stars glittered in a way she'd never seen them do before. Even so, their shining beauty still offered little light in the vast sky.

Two tall pole lights glowed on either side of the Big Fork Inn & Eats sign. It was too dark for her to see the lake, but she sensed water was close by.

Rolling down her window, she inhaled the fresh air from the breeze. In the distance, she could hear the sounds that traveled from the gentle tide.

Sam slowly continued around to the back of the inn.

As she passed through the empty lot, her headlights provided enough brightness to see some of the big two-story house that served as the inn.

Large windows fronted the bottom half and above them several smaller windows lined the top part of the house.

Sam mashed the brake pedal and idled there for a minute as she marveled at the big building. So this was the diner, and for the next year, her home.

She caught a glimpse of the double doors by the indirect glow of light from her car. Her vision followed the beam to the front of the white brick building. Her heart fluttered just a little. The charm certainly pulled a person in.

Although she'd made up her mind not to like Big Fork Lake, she couldn't deny that she sensed an unusual peace here.

Yet, she knew the real reason was simply that she was away from Atlanta, far from her troubles.

Sam guided her car slowly toward the back, noticing the five smaller units that bordered each side of the inn. Observing the doors as best as she could in the dark, she took note that each appeared to be a different color with a number painted on the front.

Sam reached the rear part of the inn, which opened to wide, unoccupied sky. In amazement, she stared at the twinkling stars again.

The luminosity of the shimmering dots overwhelmed her, the glow creating a beautiful picture that pulled her in.

Getting out of the car, exuberance grabbed her. Strong, elated emotions caught her off guard and without thought, she spun in a circle.

This was her new life!

Sam stopped suddenly, mentally adding, *for the next year anyway*.

She stared back up to the shining clusters, wishing she knew what lie ahead.

She remembered Bo always said Jesus was a help and comfort to all who would seek him. Now she hoped he would show her some of the kindness he had given Bo.

It was time to explore her new living quarters. Hopefully they were suitable, though she couldn't imagine Bo living anyway unpleasant.

Hesitating, Sam laid her hand on the railing that led to her apartment and rubbed the wood, feeling the roughness under her palm.

She lifted her foot slowly and stepped up.

As if she was in a daze, Sam climbed the stairs one at a time, wondering what the apartment she planned to call home for the next year was like. Was it comfortable? Would she have furniture? A nice kitchen?

As long as she had a decent oven to bake her pizza in, she supposed she'd be content.

Sam's throat tightened as she ascended the steps, remembering Bo once walked on the planks she was now treading.

She paused at the top of the stairs in front of the entryway. With the keys clutched in her grasp, she unlocked the door.

Sam stepped inside the door, engulfed with fond memories of her friend.

Her mind flooded as she remembered Bo and how he would gently take hold of her hands and tell her that God would walk with her, if only she let Him. She recalled a particular conversation they once had when she told him God stole everyone from her. She could still remember the expression on his face. First he looked at her in shock, then kindness. He quoted a verse out of the Bible. She didn't recall the words—it was something about being blessed if you mourn. Then he told her everyone had an appointed time and that the Lord wasn't being mean to her—God loved her.

Sam walked into the big clearing. Her eyes followed the large room. The dining and living area gave way to an open floor plan. A large kitchen island separated the two vicinities.

In a leisurely pace, Sam ambled over to the long bar and stroked her hand over the cold, black granite.

As she stood there, she grinned at the well-kept room.

The living quarters weren't anything grand, but nice and homey, just like Bo.

Suddenly, a burst of energy rushed through her. Sam dashed around and surveyed everything in the big living area, exploring the two rooms and opening cedar cabinets. The furnishings, although several years old, had a cozy appeal and were still in good condition.

She couldn't wait to sit on the overstuffed couch and sip coffee.

On the other side of the room, a fireplace stood against the far wall. Beside the cozy hearth was a tall bookcase that featured a television.

Sam gazed at the big black box with welcoming relief. She did enjoy her television and remembered that Bo liked to watch certain programs as well.

Mentally, she already planned to place her little one in the bedroom.

Sam drew her attention to the curved opening that proceeded down a long hall.

With more determination, she picked up speed and glided down the hallway. There were two doors on one side of the hall. Another entry was located on the opposite side and a larger door stood alone, regal at the end of the walkway.

Sam pushed through the door to the left and found what appeared to be the master suite. The room was painted tan with a four-poster bed that presided in the center of the room. A bathroom matched the bedroom with an extra space where a stacked washer and dryer rested.

To the right was a smaller bedroom. The color happened to be one of her favorite shades. She turned around and smiled at the way the jade painted walls pleased her.

Warmth spread over Sam as she walked into the doorway of the final room. As she looked around the room, a calming sensation of peace flooded her. Her focus went to a petite fireplace situated at the end wall facing the bed.

Sam walked over and grabbed hold of the mantel.

She could hardly wait to lie in bed while she enjoyed the glow from a toasty fire.

The room was styled more contemporary than the other bedroom, the bed framed in white, with furniture to match. Beside the bed, she noticed a door that connected the hall bath.

As Sam walked around the room, a sensation of total serenity covered her like a blanket.

At that moment, she felt as if all her troubles vanished. Sam knew this room would be her bedroom, her special retreat at night.

At the end of the hallway, she stared at the last door.

Sam turned the knob and focused on steps that led downstairs to the lobby of the inn.

She flipped the light at the top of the stairs and descended the polished wood into the space where the business was located. As she searched the big room, Sam caught sight of the office on the side, closest to the staircase.

Slowly, she turned on the light and moved into the ordinary room with a desk and computer, an old gray file cabinet, and small table. The only thing that stood out was the shelf with all the fishing memorabilia on display.

Sam switched off the light and stepped back into the area that served as a diner.

Standing in the middle, she took a quick glimpse around. A door, she assumed, led to the kitchen. The eating area itself shined with blues, maroons and browns with a lake theme painted on one wall.

Suddenly, Sam's exhaustion returned vigorously. She slightly took notice of the long bar and stools that ran the length of the counter. She sleepily observed the room, barely aware of tables and booths that lined each of the two walls.

On a winded huff of defeat, she turned to head back up the stairs.

Although Sam was tired, she was amazed that Bo did all this. Never would she have guessed that he ran an inn. A stab of guilt hit her again as she wondered why she always thought he came to the convention as a sales representative for some company.

Monday morning, Noah parked his truck outside the inn.

As he slid from his seat, his mind drifted to Bo, the way the older man had changed his life. If it hadn't been for Bo, he would probably be a different person. Bo taught him that a man did a good day's work and his strength always came from trusting in the Lord.

Noah also had Bo to thank for taking the time to teach a young man barely out of high school how to make wise financial investments.

Noah marched into Big Fork Inn & Eats. He still had a hard time visiting the establishment. Things just weren't the same without Bo. Last he heard, some lawyer finally contacted the guy who inherited the place from Bo. He tossed names around. Yeah, he believed the man's name was Sam.

Noah spotted Anne at the counter and smiled. "Hi Anne, where's Belle?"

Anne picked up the coffee pot. "Oh, she hasn't come in yet. Can I get you something, Noah?"

He sat down at the long counter, his gaze shifting to the stairs where his friend always entered. "I'll have a cup of coffee and a blueberry muffin."

Noah focused his attention on Anne. "So tell me, have you met this Sam yet?"

In her favorite yellow smock, Anne wiped the counter. "No, I haven't. When I arrived here this morning, I saw a Volkswagen Bug out back, so I guess he's upstairs. Noah, can you believe he has a Bug? Why on earth would a guy want to drive a little yellow car?" Pouring coffee, Anne's face twisted as she maintained her conversation. "Something else gets me too. For the life of me, I can't figure why Bo would leave the place to someone from out of town. Just doesn't seem right for a stranger to be taking over."

Noah sipped his coffee while he listened to Anne. He'd known Anne for many years, ever since he'd begun helping Bo at the inn as a teenager. He really couldn't say he knew a lot about her life, but still, he liked and respected her.

"Anne, Bo realized what he was doing, I don't understand why he left the place to this Sam either, but Bo was smarter than we're giving him credit for."

He continued to examine Anne over his cup, noticing the faraway look of sadness that drifted across her face. "Anne, you have to remember Sam wasn't a stranger to Bo. He was Bo's friend and we have to respect that."

"I just never expected him to go like that. I miss him more than you know."

Noah laid his hand on Anne's hand. "I know, Anne. I don't think Bo ever realized how much you cared for him."

Anne made a show of smoothing down her apron. "I guess after Dale died it was just natural for me to grow fond of Bo. We worked together all those years. Nevertheless, I still don't know about his decision to leave the inn to this Sam person. I hope Bo made the right choice. Anyway, Noah, you are right—Bo was a smart man and Sam was his friend. I'll get used to things."

Noah took the last drink of his coffee and slid off the stool.

"Anne, just put a muffin in a bag. I have to go. I'll stop back by later."

Sam woke and lazily stretched. Her nose picked up the smell of fresh brewed coffee and she inhaled, savoring the fragrance.

She sat on the side of the bed and looked around the room.

Her sight settled on the fireplace. Already, she was more rested than she had been in months.

Puttering around in her boxes, she dug out her clothes. Being away from her old neighborhood for just one night apparently made a big difference. She felt ready to tackle anything today.

Sam gathered her things and took a glimpse quickly out the window. She wasn't about to consciously admit just how good she felt being here at the inn. This was only an escape and for that, she was grateful.

As she headed to the bathroom, she stuffed any other notions that began to surface back down, deep inside. She planned to make the best of the situation then she could figure out where she wanted to live the rest of her life.

Sam showered as she speculated on places—maybe she'd sell out and move to Florida. She had always liked the beach, so maybe she could find a place close to water. That way, she could spend her free time lounging in the sun.

Forty minutes later, Sam was dressed in corduroy slacks, ready to go downstairs and meet the women. As she jogged down the steps to the inn's diner, she spied an older lady wearing glasses who appeared to be about Bo's age talking to a young woman sporting a long ponytail.

The lady in the glasses peeped up at Sam and her face immediately paled. Her coffee plummeted to the ground. Coffee puddled on the floor.

In an instant, the younger woman rushed to her side with a towel.

Sam gasped as she stepped off the last stair and hurried over to help. "Oh, are you all right?"

The older woman glared up at Sam from her bent position. "Who are you?" she demanded.

The woman's face took on an odd, almost threatening expression.

Sam smiled and tried to put the woman at ease. "My name is Samantha Blacker. I was Bo's friend from Atlanta." Putting out her hand, she extended a greeting. "Please, call me Sam."

The younger woman stared with curiosity and approached. "Hi Sam, I'm Belle. I'm the waitress here. This is Anne—she's the cook and has always made the best desserts."

Sam nodded her head in agreement at Anne. "Yes, Bo told me about your pecan pie. He said no one could make it better."

The older woman's face transformed from shock to pride. "Bo always did like my desserts. So...you're Sam Blacker. Mr. Wright did tell us you were coming, but all he said was Sam Blacker would be arriving. I guess we expected a man."

Sam smiled, thinking that would indeed be a shock. "Sorry about that. It's good to meet both of you."

The younger woman flashed a warm smile. "I am sure we will work together just fine. I'm glad to see you are finally here."

Anne watched Sam, the uncertainty obvious on her face. "Sam, do you know anything about running an inn?"

Sam walked behind the counter and went to the coffee pot.

She picked up an empty cup. "Yes, some. I'm sure I'll get into the routine of things easy enough. I have various types of experience."

Anne smiled and wobbled her head. "That's good. We all pitch in around here—at least, when Bo was here we did."

Sam poured herself a cup of coffee, shaking her head. "I don't see why that should change, Anne."

Anne and Belle showed her around and familiarized her with where everything was located. She spent most of the day going over the books and becoming familiar with the names of some local people in town.

She found Bo's notebook in the desk with assorted information on the daily running of the inn and a list of phone numbers. She made phone calls to different places that the inn did business with and informed them she would be handling things now.

That afternoon, Sam ambled over to the window in the office. She longed to walk outside and tour the cabins. The day had flown by far too fast for her.

Gazing at the clock on the wall, Sam decided to wait and see the lodge rooms tomorrow.

In the quiet after Anne and Belle left, she leisurely strolled around the inn's dining room.

She checked over anything she may have missed earlier and used the time to examine the kitchen. She enjoyed seeing everything at her own pace.

As Sam headed back upstairs to her apartment, a bit of pride managed to sneak past her defenses. For the first time in a long while, she enjoyed being tired and the satisfaction of a job well done.

That night a deep sleep overtook Sam. She rested soundly for the first time in months.

No worries about a job and thank goodness, there was no Rob roaming the halls. So far, all was good.

The weekend provided Sam a chance to explore the cabins and clean them.

She also got to chat with a few of the locals that stopped in. Each one offered stories of Bo and wished her the best at the inn. As she went through the cabins, she realized the doors were painted a different color and adorned with room numbers and the color of the cabin's interior turned out to be the same as the entrance.

The small baths in every room held all the necessities for a comfortable stay.

Sam was still in awe that Bo managed all this. She now realized there was a lot about Bo she had taken for granted.

Sam woke up early Sunday morning anxious to put her touch to the apartment. Thank goodness Bo had always closed the inn on Sundays—it gave her a day to rest. That was certainly something she didn't plan on changing. She unpacked, cleaned and rearranged the furniture. While searching through the closets, she found a hammer and some nails to hang a few of the pictures she brought with her.

She passed the afternoon by lounging on the overstuffed sofa.

She gazed across the room at the crackling fire, glad the weather was still chilly so she could use the brick fireplace.

Her eyes moved to the long mantel above the fire where she placed a statue—the same miniature horse that she used to defend herself against Rob. Without it, who knew what might have happened? She guessed now it was her lucky charm.

Smiling, Sam recalled a memory of her grandmother holding the horse. Grandma always had a fondness for those big animals. That little statue was the only item that survived the fire.

Comfortable with her hot chocolate, she watched the fire crackle and snap. Sam soaked in the relaxing atmosphere of peace that encompassed her. She shifted her weight and put her legs under her.

Why did being in this apartment conjure up a tranquility that seemed to spread through her? She wondered if the reason was because she was away from Atlanta. Could she really *like* this place?

Her sight moved around the room. She couldn't remember ever having lived anywhere that gave her the contentment she was experiencing at this moment. A sense of being where she was supposed to be, she thought.

No, that wasn't the reason. She'd worked all day getting the apartment the way she wanted. She was tired and the warmth of the fire relaxed her—that was all.

Sam traveled back a few days to her conversations with some of the local people. Despite all, she liked them. In fact, they weren't at all as she'd expected—simple, hicks...nosy. Just friendly, welcoming and warm people.

The simplicity of life in a small town did put things in a different perspective. Sam stretched out on the sofa and closed her eyes. No, she was a city girl at heart.

Early Monday morning, Sam was eager to start a new day. Anne called and explained she'd be a little late. Sam told her not to worry—she would get the coffee going and start a batch of pastries.

Armed with her goal, Sam headed downstairs to get things ready. She really needed to learn the routine in the kitchen before the tourist season began anyway. After all, the inn was her responsibility now...at least for a year.

Just as Sam pulled out a second batch of muffins, the door chimed. She wiped her hands on her apron as she stepped out of the kitchen to the counter.

Across the room, Sam stared at the county health inspector.

Stopping in her tracks, she silently hoped everything would be up to code. She hadn't even considered the fact that having a diner and inn meant monthly inspections.

She tried to center her attention on the inn and any impending situations that could arise, but her mind would not cooperate. Instead, her focus landed on the good-looking man with the county logo on his shirt.

Tingles tiptoed down her spine as she tried to shake off the attraction.

Mindlessly, she laid her hand on her throat and wet her dry lips. When was the last time a man awoke such awareness in her?

As the inspector moved about, Sam scolded herself. First off, he was here to inspect and that was all. Second was the fact that she didn't need to become involved with any man. Especially not in Big Fork Lake—this was just a temporary stop for her.

No, she absolutely would not notice how his white work shirt stretched across his broad chest. Nor was she going to pay any attention to those locks of thick wavy hair.

As Sam wiped her hands on a towel and leaned on the counter, she scanned ahead of the inspector. Her eyes fell on anything she thought would distract her.

Uncontrollably, her eyes moved back and lingered on his body.

She couldn't stop herself from wondering what it would feel like to run her fingers through his hair and push back the tresses that had fallen across his forehead.

Noah finished his inspection of the kitchen and the restrooms and paced his steps as he walked toward the counter with his clipboard. He knew just about everyone in Big Fork Lake, but didn't remember seeing this woman around. She must be kin to the new owner, he figured.

His senses turned on him as he ogled the petite woman. She was certainly something to feast eyes on. Noah's vision moved down the length of her body—oh yeah, she definitely could get his attention anytime.

He shook off the mental picture of the material of her sweater clinging to her chest and forced his sight to move to her face.

Noah slowly wobbled his head, resolved to stand unmoved by her.

He had a job to do. He didn't have time to dwell on someone with captivating blue eyes that seeped right into his soul. Maybe later, he told himself, when he had time for distraction.

He approached the counter and noticed she wasn't wearing a ring on her finger. A surge of longing crept up—at least she wasn't married.

Seconds passed and Noah's breath caught in his chest and his gaze traveled her face and strolled to the ends of her hair.

Finally, finding his voice, he spoke. "I'm looking for Sam."

The woman shined a big smile his way and nodded toward the clipboard.

"I'm Sam. Do I need to sign that?"

Noah handed Sam the inspection sheet as his face turned a shade whiter. "*You're* Sam?"

"Yes, I'm Samantha Blacker, but everyone calls me Sam."

She signed with a flourish as Noah searched his mind for the right words.

"So, you're Bo's friend from Atlanta." He tried to remember if Bo ever said anything about his visits to Atlanta that might include the fact that Sam was a woman. Had his friend been seeing someone?

Bo was a Christian with strong values, but Noah had to admit that a woman such as this could confuse a man.

For now, he decided to give the situation the benefit of doubt and held out his hand. "Sam, I'm Noah Frye, one of Bo's friends."

Sam smiled and accepted his grasp in a small shake.

Noah jerked back his hand. His body turned against him, telling him to caress the tender flesh and let the softness of her skin comfort him.

No, he was going to find out what kind of friend Sam was to Bo. Noah quickly pointed to a space she missed initialing on the paperwork. "Well, Sam this is just a small place and there's not much to offer, not like the big city."

Sam penned *SB* on a dotted line and handed the clipboard back to Noah. "That may be just the change I need for now. It's good to meet you, Noah. Bo said you were like a son to him."

Satisfaction swelled in Noah. "Yes, he changed my life. Bo was very special to me."

A relaxed mood covered Sam as the conversation started to ease the sexual tension. "Can I get you a cup of coffee? On the house, of course."

Sam watched as Noah's expression spiraled into something Sam couldn't place. A total change came about and he raised his voice. "I pay for my stuff here at the inn."

Shocked by the outburst, Sam stepped back a little. "I'm sorry. I didn't mean to imply anything. I thought—"

Noah glared, his face reddening. "You thought because I'm the inspector you have to bribe me with coffee."

Confusion hit Sam head on. "No, I didn't mean anything by that, Mr. Frye. I thought Bo would do that."

Noah's penetrating look grew cold. "No, Bo did not do that. He never bribed me. He always kept the inn up to code and as long as you do the same, Ms. Blacker, we will not have a problem. Unless you prefer to bribe people to get what you want?"

Sam bustled with alarm, astonished by his words. A kick in the teeth wouldn't have hurt as bad as his low opinion. More than offended, Sam was infuriated with this man. How dare he presume to know what kind of woman she was?

As Sam narrowed her eyes at Noah in dismay, her hands flew to her hips and she stood poised for battle.

Biting her lip, she spat out, "How *dare* you say something like that to me? You don't even know me! I was only trying to be nice, Mr. Frye. For goodness sake, I only offered you a cup of coffee, not a five-course meal!"

Swiftly, Noah felt gilded. Her heated response surprised him.

Deep down, he realized that his retort sounded inappropriate. Forcing control, he pushed down his temper.

A thought quickly surfaced in his mind of how the Bible speaks about judging. He remembered a verse in Matthew. He certainly didn't want to be judged for his mistakes so why was he being so quick to criticize this woman?

He drew a long breath, calming himself. "I'm sorry. Please, call me Noah. We've gotten off to a bad start. I made presumptions and I shouldn't have said that to you."

Sam scrutinized his face. Finally, she moved closer to the counter and offered the beginning of an uncertain smile.

Noah flashed a grin back at her. "Sam, I'm truly sorry I was so unfriendly. Bo spoke about a friend in Atlanta named Sam, but he never mentioned you were a woman. I expected to meet a man."

"I'm getting a lot of that lately." Sam laughed lightly as she tucked a wayward strand of hair behind her ear. "Now can I get you a cup of coffee?"

Noah flashed a bigger smile and shook his head. "Of course. Please."

Even with the confrontation, Noah still warred with his flesh.

Watching Sam pour his coffee, he rubbed his face, trying to remove the image that burned in his mind.

He would not let his eyes linger on her curves. After all, the question now was what was her real relationship with Bo?

Maybe he needed to find out a little more about this Sam.

Just then, Anne walked in swinging her big gold purse.

Sam glanced up from pouring the coffee and silently blew out a breath, relieved for the diversion. She needed to step away from this man.

"Hi Anne, I'm glad you're here. I've another batch of muffins in the oven and sliced roast beef for lunch. I need to go to the office and finish the books and check on the supplies."

Sam placed the coffee down on the counter and offered a gesture of goodbye to Noah.

Noah silently watched her walk away. She was the first woman in a long time to create such emotions in him.

Anne broke his concentration by noisily sitting a muffin in front of him.

Noah quickly turned his head, embarrassed to be caught watching Sam walk into her office.

"Anne, what do you make of Sam?"

Anne glanced toward the office door and lowered her voice. "I can't say. You know I trusted Bo's judgment...sometimes I just don't understand why things happen the way they do."

Noah sipped his coffee as he continued, "Do you know how close she and Bo were?"

Anne turned to make more coffee. "They were just friends as

far as I can figure. She hasn't said a lot about that yet."

Sam stayed busy all through the day, compelled by a driving force that seemed to push her.

In the back of her mind, she kept reminding herself this was only for a year. Despite her resolve, she would still find herself unwillingly yielding to a sense that she belonged here. She felt an attachment to the inn that she tried not to acknowledge.

The next morning, Sam emerged from her shower prepared to face another day. She actually looked forward to working at the inn.

While Sam took inventory in the storage room, she listened as Anne and Belle prepared the pastries and lined up cups for coffee.

The door opened and Sam heard heavy footsteps fill the diner. A strong voice seeped with a deep southern accent broke into the women's routine.

"Belle, can I have a cup of that coffee?"

"Sure, Sheriff."

As Sam stepped out of the back room, she faced the largest man she'd ever seen before.

Belle shined her perky smile in Sam's direction. "This is Sheriff Gruver, Sam."

Sheriff Gruver's disapproving glare hit Sam like a slap in the face.

Sam approached the sheriff, determined to be friendly. "Hi Sheriff! I'm Samantha Blacker, but please, call me Sam."

Sheriff Gruver was determined not to allow this woman to charm him. "Good to meet you. So you're Bo's 'friend' from Atlanta?"

The big man watched Sam's reaction. He couldn't help but question whether there was more to the story that he needed to find out. "I hear Bo left you this place. Can't help but wonder why he would will his home and business to someone who lived so far away. A stranger to all. Of course, only you know the reason for that."

Sam was bewildered by the tone he used and the remark he made. "Sheriff, Bo and I were good friends. I suppose that's why he wanted me to take over the inn."

Sheriff Gruver made little attempt to hide his scorn. "So you were 'just friends,' huh little darlin'? Excuse me, *ladies*, but I have a call to go on."

Rising, the sheriff avoided her face as he tossed money on the counter and turned to rush out the door.

Sam looked over at Belle as she wiped up the counter and gave her a questioning stare. "Belle, why in the world did he say those things? Is he always that way with strangers?"

Belle shook her head in wonder and replied, "I'm not sure, Sam. He was a little rude."

On Friday, Sam spent time making notes for some ideas for the inn. She sighed as she reread the list, hoping the girls would like some of the modifications she planned to make.

Certainly, they could use a little more organization around the place. As much as she respected Bo, the diner could be better managed.

She came out of her office and glanced around, shaking off any sense of contentment that tried to squeeze beyond her guard. "Anne and Belle, when we close today I'd like to see you both. We're going to make some changes. I'll be back in a few hours. I have to go to town for a while."

The ladies watched as Sam strolled into the parking lot. Belle couldn't help but wonder. "Anne, what do you think she means by changes?"

Anne nodded her head as she intently focused on the now closed door Sam walked through. "I don't know, but I guess we'll find out soon enough."

Sam slid into her little car and headed into town. While she drove the few miles to Main Street, she took pleasure in the way the cars moved sedately toward their destinations.

She didn't hear any honking horns or deal with any vehicles rushing to cut her off. Instead, Sam listened to the thrashing sounds that the lake made and watched birds flying over. The rhythmic whipping of water beckoned to her. She peered beyond the short distance to the lake that flowed beside the town.

When Sam spotted a billboard similar to one she remembered back in Atlanta, her mind revisited her old hometown neighborhood. Mentally, she compared the differences in Alabama to Atlanta, Georgia.

She abstractly picked out all the good things about Big Fork Lake. Suddenly, the fact that she favored the slower paced town and the family atmosphere struck her.

As she admired children playing in the much smaller park, Sam realized what she was doing and couldn't help but wonder what it meant for her.

Could she really prefer this little rural town to the city?

After her accounts were all set up and contracts signed at the bank, Sam decided to walk around and do some sightseeing.

She strolled down the sidewalk and soaked in the storefronts and the habitat. The big oaks were starting to bud and she spotted an old building that held a sign on the front shaped like a hammer with the words "Artie's Hardware" stenciled on the side.

With a contented pace, she crossed the street, spying several other small merchant shops scattered around. Her attention landed on a checkered curtain in one window of a small country diner. Beside the diner was a blue and yellow building with an ice cream cone painted on one window.

Happily, she marched toward the small shop, drawn to the little storefront.

Sam was relieved to find the ice cream shop. Her last thought before she passed through the bright blue door was of a chocolate milkshake.

Inside, Sam gaped, feeling as if she stepped back in time...back to memories of a small ice cream shop she frequented with her mom.

This little room was decorated with the same yellow metal tables and chairs as her long-ago memory. Sitting in the corner, Sam stared fondly at the jukebox.

After she placed an order with the young waiter, she rushed over to the box and rubbed her hand across the old glass, reading the titles for the music listed.

Punching in B-five, she listened to some beach music and soaked in the coziness that covered her like a pair of fuzzy bedroom slippers.

While she savored her milkshake, she pretended she was in another place at a different time.

At eight, Sam turned over the open sign to close and seated herself with Anne and Belle at a corner table. Glancing around the inn, she fondly noted the counter with the pastries and one table to the side of the room that still needed cleared.

Her vision landed on the fishing scene painted on the wall. Belonging ascended in Sam and pricked her emotions.

She shook off the feeling. Was that something she wanted to acknowledge?

Sam noticed Anne and Belle fidgeting nervously and put forth a positive attitude to help the uneasy situation. "Okay ladies, let's try to make the inn easier to manage."

Anne glanced at Sam wearing an uncertain expression. "I think things are fine."

Sam expected a reaction like that and knew she had to stand firm in her decisions. "Well some changes are necessary and will save money."

She ignored the scowling countenance on Anne's face as the woman narrowed her eyes toward Sam. Glancing at Belle, Sam was saddened by the look of uncertainty that shown in her eyes.

The young woman was easy going. She did a good job and was always helpful. Sam wanted them both to know she was not out to make things difficult.

Sam folded her hands on the table and plastered a smile on her lips. "You know, I was shocked when I discovered Bo left me this place. I really didn't know he owned an inn."

After a pause she continued, hoping if she opened up a little about her friendship with Bo the ladies would feel more at ease around her.

"He came to Atlanta for the restaurant convention every year and we would talk and have lunch together. For five years, Bo was my friend. I know you may think it's odd that we were friends, but Bo was like an uncle to me. He always listened to my latest gripe." With a saddened grin, she added, "He would always tell me a Bible story or scripture to help me."

Shaking the memory off, Sam shrugged her shoulders and focused on the present. "I assumed he worked for a supplier or something."

Belle gazed at Sam in amazement. "You mean all those years you never knew he owned the inn?"

Sam's gaze darted back and forth between the ladies and she shook her head. "No, I guess I was the one who did most of the talking. We shared about our personal lives a little, but not much. Looking back, I realize now that I had many preconceptions about Bo. He spent most of his conversations talking to me about Jesus. I was shocked when I found out he was gone and really stunned when the lawyer told me he left this place to me."

Sam paused, watching both women. "I know Bo was a levelheaded man and I know that he wouldn't have left me this place if he didn't think I could handle running it."

As Anne lifted her gaze toward Sam, her face softened. "No, I guess not, Sam. Bo was a smart man."

Relief flooded Sam and gave her the courage to finish with her plans. "Good. Let's work together to make this the best place we can for Bo's memory."

Belle's ponytail swung in the air as she nodded. "Okay, I'll do what I can to help."

Turning a page in her notebook, Sam glanced down at her notes. "I know you will, Belle, you are very helpful. Your hours will stay the same except on Mondays—from this day forward you get that off."

Sam saw her face brighten as if she had won the lottery.

Sam turned her attention toward Anne. She scanned Anne's face and realized Anne was older than she appeared. She couldn't help but guess that her appearance was the result of living in a small town. "I noticed you do a lot around here, Anne."

Anne spoke up quickly. "Yes and I've never minded. I always tried to help Bo out."

Understanding what Anne was saying, Sam continued, "Yes, I know Anne—you do the cooking and clean the rooms. You do a good job. It's just that it's a lot for you to do in the busy season."

Anne wasn't sure what Sam was getting at. She certainly wasn't ready to retire yet. Defensively, she blurted, "I don't mind and Belle helps with the rooms. Bo wasn't any good at cleaning, so I always have."

Sam appreciated Anne's willingness, but for some reason, she needed to take on more of the responsibilities of running the inn. "I'm always just upstairs, so I'll work on Saturdays with Belle. This way both of you will have two consecutive days off."

"I'll also start cleaning the rooms after lunch on Thursdays so they are ready in time for Friday check-ins. That keeps you free so you can do some extra cooking. We need to cook ahead and freeze some of the desserts for the busy season."

Scanning her notes one last time, Sam added, "We'll also be getting some vending machines to place outside for the guests."

Anne fidgeted with her fingernails. "I'm not sure, Sam. Bo always liked the food fresh and vending machines...I don't understand the need for them."

Sam was determined to stick to her guns and show the girls she now ran the inn. "We need vending machines, Anne. That way, the guests will be able to get a snack late night when the diner is closed." Gently, Sam reminded them, "Bo is not here now. I am and I need to make these changes. These few things will cut down on the need to stay late sometimes. I'll go to the bank around three in the afternoon instead of the morning. I'd rather the money get into the bank for the night."

She quickly observed the late time on the clock and figured everything that needed said had been, for now.

With an irrevocable determination in her voice, she ended the meeting.

While Sam returned to the confines of the office, Anne turned her head toward Belle and whispered, "I hope she knows what she is doing. Making all these changes?"

Belle shrugged. "I know Anne, but she may have some good ideas."

Anne's face crinkled, showing uncertainty. "Yes, of course you would think that. You'll still get the tips from Saturday. It's good that I draw from my husband's stock fund, but that money won't last me forever. And vending machines are so tacky. I understand she means well, but I'm just uncertain."

Belle nodded her head. She liked the older lady, but often didn't understand her ways. Laying her hand on Anne's shoulder, she spoke gently. "Anne, everything will be all right. Sam seems like she has some good ideas."

Anne stared at Belle and wished she could make her understand why she felt unsure. "I suppose I've never been good with change. I just need to get use to things being different now."

CHAPTER FIVE

The next two weeks came and went with things going pretty much the way Sam wanted them to. She was glad she changed the routine around. The inn seemed to run smoother.

Saturday morning came and Sam busied herself warming blueberry muffins and making coffee when Noah strolled in.

"Good morning Sam, where are Anne and Belle?"

Sam selected a clean cup and ignored the nagging sensation of excitement at seeing Noah. She was determined not to heed to the jittery nerves that crawled across her stomach just because he sat at the counter.

Mentally, she scolded herself because of the nervous flutters in her stomach. "I've changed the schedule. I open and close the inn on Saturdays now. Belle comes in at eleven and leaves at five.

Noah turned his head quickly, hoping Sam hadn't noticed him staring at her. He found it hard not to gaze into her big blue eyes. "Well, I guess I'll have a banana muffin and cup of coffee."

The sheriff marched in and looked toward Noah. "Morning, Noah. Where are the other ladies?"

Noah placed his coffee cup down. "Sam changed the hours. Belle will be in later."

The sheriff managed to nod his head slightly in a greeting at Sam. "Is that so? I guess things do change."

Sam handed him a cup of coffee. Even though she was unsure about the sheriff, she remained unwavering in her response. "Please, Sheriff, call me Sam."

Sheriff Gruver barely glanced her way then turned his attention to Noah. "Noah, come sit down over at the window with me a minute."

They moved to a booth by the wall and Noah slid in the seat. The big man scooted in across from him and lowered his voice as he started to talk. "Noah, what do you know about her?"

Taken by surprise at the sound of doubt in his voice, Noah studied the sheriff. "Nothing...just that she was Bo's friend. According to Bo, she'd seen some bad luck in life, but he believed she was a good person at heart."

Sheriff Gruver stared out the window and mumbled before he responded. "I don't know. Something just doesn't seem right to me."

Sam came to the table with a refill for their coffee. "Can I get you anything else, Sheriff?"

Abruptly, he looked Sam up and down and gave her a fast answer. "No thanks, I have to go."

Noah sat in the vinyl seat wondering why the sheriff was acting this way. He never remembered him treating someone new this way before.

As he sipped his coffee, he recalled what the Bible said about how we should treat each other and not cast stones, even though we may be different.

Sam slowly moved about cleaning tables, gradually working her way toward Noah's booth.

Noah smiled at Sam. "So, how do you like being here in Big Fork?"

Sam stopped washing the tabletop and flashed a grin toward Noah.

"You know, at first I thought I wouldn't like this little town. I've always been a city girl, but the area isn't so bad. Actually, it's nice not hearing all the street noise."

Sam left Noah to his thoughts and returned a few minutes later with another refill.

Unable to resist, she poured coffee and encouraged more small talk. "Have you lived here all your life?"

Noah rolled his eyes nonchalantly. "Even attended Montgomery Community College."

Intrigued, Sam responded, "You never wanted to be anywhere else?"

With a catch in his voice, he replied, "No, can't say I have."

The eye contact between them made Sam shift on her feet uncomfortably. "Almost everyone has given me a chance except a couple folks."

"You mean the sheriff."

"Yes, along with Anne. Sometimes I think she resents me taking over the inn." With a shrug, Sam turned to walk off.

In a sudden haste not to let her go, Noah said, "She'll come around in time. She just misses Bo. I think Anne has always had a hard time trusting people."

Noah swiped his hair back and felt the hole in his heart from the loss of his friend. "You know, I hope you make things work out for you here, Sam."

Sam cocked her head intently at Noah with a little skepticism. "Do you really, Noah?"

Seeing the doubt in her eyes made him feel troubled. Somewhere deep inside, Noah did want Sam to succeed. "Sam, if Bo thought you could handle running an inn, I have to believe that also. Bo knew what he was doing."

Sam smiled with a grin that brightened her entire face. "Noah, thank you for saying that."

She turned to walk away again when Noah's hand lightly touched her arm. "Have you been to Big Fork Fish Camp yet?"

Startled, Sam studied Noah and bid herself not to pay any attention to the tingling sensation his hand created. "No, actually...I haven't. I heard about the food there though. Seems to be a popular place to eat around here."

Noah's hand still rested on her arm as he asked, "What time are you closing?"

Without realizing why, Sam rushed an answer. "At seven on Saturdays."

Noah moved his hand as he slowly asked, "Would you go? I mean with me, Sam?"

Sam took a quivering breath, contemplating her answer. Her head spun with his words. Her mind wrestled with his question.

Apprehension seeped up as she remembered the last time she went out with someone. Look what trouble that caused her.

Noah frowned. "Sam, is everything all right?"

Struggling for an answer, she remembered that she did say this was a new start for her. Sam shyly responded, "Yes, Noah, I think I would like that."

Before Noah could change his mind, he added, "I'll come by and pick you up at eight. The fish house stays open late on Saturdays."

All day, Sam played out the date in her mind. She fussed at her decision. She could only hope she was doing the right thing.

At seven, Sam closed up and quickly climbed the stairs to her apartment. After getting out of her bath, she struggled with what to wear.

She hadn't gone out with anyone she was this attracted to in a long time. Regardless, she only hoped she wasn't making a mistake.

Sam tossed sweaters out of her drawer as she tried to decide what to wear. She slid hanger after hanger in her closet. Taking a survey of her clothes, she recognized for the first time that her wardrobe was more suited for Big Fork Lake than for living in Atlanta anyway.

Funny, she never noticed that about her clothes before. Maybe deep in her heart, she was a country girl after all.

She settled for a blue-jean skirt that hung just above the knee and a pink V-neck sweater.

Not long after, Sam spotted him out her window as he pulled in her driveway in his tan pick-up. Curiously, she watched Noah as he parked. Deep inside, she guessed she was waiting for something out of the ordinary.

How did a girl really know? Would the right man somehow seem different? Such questions bothered her at times and she couldn't help but wonder if all women went through such uncertainty.

Noah turned off his engine and glanced at the steps that led to Sam's apartment.

This was the first time in a long time that he was actually nervous about a date. He exited the driver's side of his pickup as Sam floated down the steps. "Hi. You sure look pretty."

Noah opened the truck door for Sam.

Sam stood there a second, surprised, lost in the wonder of a man who would be so polite. No one ever held a door for her. That was something she only saw in the movies. Yes, things were different in Big Fork Lake.

On the drive to the fish camp, Noah showed Sam some of the local sites and gave her a little history of the town. She relaxed beside Noah, her nervousness forgotten, and took in all he shared.

Never did she realize that she'd enjoy a history lesson so much, but she hung on to every word that rolled off his tongue as she bathed in the melody of his husky voice.

Sam knew by the way he talked about Big Fork Lake that he loved this town.

Sitting next to him in the truck, she watched the scenery whiz by and suddenly realized that change wasn't always a bad thing.

Sam told Noah about her grandmother who raised her. She recounted some details about her mom.

Noah talked more, this time about his life with Bo as his mentor. He also spoke a bit about his mother and how hard she worked after his dad died, always keeping up with the household expenses, supporting him in school sports and making sure he went to church at least most of the time.

They pulled in front of what reminded Sam of an old seed mill. Sam surveyed the building with the faded wood siding and tree-bark sign shaped like a fish. Bright red letters announced "Big Fork Fish Camp."

Sam took in the surrounding area and the rustic charm all around as Noah got out of the truck and hurried to open the door for her.

Sam smiled to herself, thinking how nice it was when a man went out of his way to make a woman feel special.

Inside the restaurant, she scanned the big room with tables and booths scattered throughout. As the hostess escorted them to a corner table, she watched in awe as he nodded and greeted folks at table after table, realizing that Noah must know just about everyone in town.

She was amazed at the contrast from big city existence to living in a town where everyone seemed to know everyone. Noah introduced her to several people, then politely held Sam's chair for her to slide into her seat before he sat down across from her.

"What do you think of the place?"

Sam laid her napkin in her lap and glanced around.

She actually did like the place. "It's great, Noah. I'm still getting use to small-town life, but I'm finding out I like being here better each day. Discovering that I enjoy listening to crickets instead of the police sirens. That sort of thing."

Noah longed to reach out and take her hand, but instead fidgeted with his silverware. "I can't imagine life anywhere else."

While Noah talked, he ignored the urge to run his hand down her smooth skin. He was attracted to Sam, even though he had some doubts about her.

During the evening, they chatted back and forth about the town and Sam's life. Every so often, Noah would ask Sam a question. As he listened, he let himself believe that she was being upfront with her answers.

As the evening moved on, any uncertainty and his fears regarding Sam and her relationship with Bo slowly slipped away.

Noah valued Bo's opinion and his good eye for character. Helping people was something Bo had always tried to do.

He couldn't find any reason to doubt his friend's judgment now.

Sam listened to him go on about the ways of small community living and wondered what it would be like to be involved with someone like him. He seemed to be honest and outspoken.

That definitely was something she hadn't encountered much.

She didn't even mind answering his questions, deep as they sometimes prodded. Maybe the fact that she was sitting there, visualizing her hands in his hair, had something to do with the way she seemed willing to offer answers so quickly. She could almost feel the texture of those curls between her fingers.

All through the night, they continued to exchange stories.

Noah expressed how Bo helped him become a man who believed in God. Sam told Noah what it was like to live in the middle of a big city. She also realized while she shared those experiences that at times she'd felt as if she didn't fit in.

On the drive back to her apartment, Sam tried to focus on the conversation and not his hand resting over hers. "Tell me about Anne. She seems to be a little untrusting at times. I've tried to be a friend to her."

Noah offered reassurance to Sam. "Oh, I wouldn't take Anne personally. Losing Bo has been hard on her...I suspect Anne was in love with Bo."

Sam pictured Bo in her mind—she could see where Anne might be attracted to him. "Bo never wanted a relationship after Elaine died."

"No, he said he was happy living the way he was and waiting on God to take him home to see Elaine. Their relationship gave me the opportunity to see how a marriage was supposed to be. Bo taught me that you have to put God first."

Sam moved her hand and glanced over at Noah with unbelief. "Noah, how can you believe like that? I mean...with all the stuff that goes on in this world?"

Noah grinned. He was comfortable talking about God, so he rushed in. "There are a lot of different answers to that, Sam. For me, I guess it means reading the Bible, having belief in what Jesus promises. You just trust God to help you along the way. Every day I keep God in mind and try to do what His word says."

Sam's mind played back to one of the last conversations she had with Bo. "Bo was always telling me to give my life to Jesus and trust in Him. I just don't know how you can trust in God when He doesn't really care anyway."

Noah gripped the steering wheel and silently asked the Lord for guidance. He couldn't just let her statement go without finding out why she felt like that. "Sam, what makes you say that?"

Sam wiggled in the seat next to Noah. She remembered the time when Bo had asked her the same question. "Noah, I never knew my father. My mother was killed in a car wreck before I was fourteen. Then four years later, I lost my grandmother to a fire. It just seems to me that if God loved us, He wouldn't put such suffering in our lives."

Noah inhaled a deep breath. "Sam, we all have a time to die. I know it doesn't seem fair. God wasn't zapping you with bad luck—it was simply their time. I can't explain the circumstances. Nevertheless, Jesus *did* protect you in His way. When your mom died, God gave your grandmother the strength to take you in and raise you. When something happened to your grandmother, you were old enough to live on your own. We are all alike, Sam. We go through bad things. That will never change. But having a relationship with Jesus makes the sorrow easier to bear. I remember the day my mom passed away. I was sick with heartache. She was my hero. Thank goodness I had Bo. He stepped in and gave me the strength to understand that life must go on. All the years I went to church, I just went to please mom. That year, I got saved."

Noah took this opportunity to ask one final question, determined that this would be the last time he worried over it. He was going to pray about the situation and put it in God's hands. "So how did you and Bo meet, Sam?"

Sam was glad the subject had been changed. As her mind traveled back, she started talking. "One day, I stopped in at a sandwich shop during my lunch hour. Bo was at the counter eating.

"He said, 'Hi'. I said, 'Hello' and before I realized, we were sitting together, enjoying our meals and talking about Atlanta. When I got up to leave, Bo told me he would be back the next year. He asked me if I would come to Baker's and have lunch with him again.

"From then on, every year we would meet at Baker's for lunch. Sometimes we would spend hours sitting at the little diner just talking.

"You know, Noah, I never was sure why I did that. I'm not the type of person who warms to people like that, but there was something special about Bo."

Noah listened and realized he was glad Sam and Bo had known each other. "Bo really cared about people, Sam."

Noah pulled up to her door, disappointed their date was over already. He rushed to the other side of the truck and opened the door for her.

Sam slid out of his truck. While she stood there beside the door, Noah bent down.

Slowly, his lips captured hers in an unhurried kiss that lingered.

Sam warmed eagerly to Noah's touch, tasting the tenderness that his lips offered.

To her disappointment, Noah pulled away gradually and eased from her lips. One last butterfly kiss on her mouth and he concentrated on tucking her hair behind her ear.

In a gruff attempt to speak, he inhaled. "Sam, I better leave. I really enjoyed having dinner with you tonight."

Still battling with the sensation of Noah's lips on hers, she reined in her emotions and struggled for words. "Bye, Noah, and thanks for asking me out. I enjoyed the dinner."

His hand moved away, reaching for Sam's, and he walked her up the steps to her apartment.

As Sam unlocked her door, he placed a kiss on her fingers and turned to go. "Sam, I'll see you Monday."

While Noah headed out of the drive, Sam closed her door.

Neither noticed the older model, dark colored truck parked in the shadows, waiting and watching.

Monday morning, Sam bounced downstairs.

Sheriff Gruver was sitting at the counter eating a muffin. Anne busied herself in the kitchen getting more coffee.

Belle, who always had a smile for Sam, waved her hand. "Hi Sam, you seem relaxed this morning."

"Thanks Belle. I haven't felt this content in a long time." She smiled. "Sheriff, it's nice to see you this morning."

Sheriff Gruver sent Sam a peculiar look and mumbled something under his breath about Sam and the town.

Sam noted his assertive pose but was determined not to let him ruin her morning. "Sheriff, you know...I'm getting use to small-town life. In fact, I like living in the country more than I believed I would. It's nice to wake up to trees all around and seeing the lake. Even to greet your grumpy face in my diner every morning."

Sheriff Gruver pushed his stool back. "Well, maybe you better not get too use to things. Never know when you might want to go back to Atlanta."

As the big man strolled out the door, he left Sam with a weird feeling. For the first time in her life, she really cared about what someone thought of her.

"Belle, why doesn't he like me?"

Wiping up a table, Belle looked over at Sam and shrugged her shoulder. "I don't know, Sam. *I* like you. The sheriff has always been suspicious of new people, I guess."

Anne stepped out of the kitchen in time to hear the last part of their conversation. "Just give him time, Sam. I'm sure he'll come around."

Sam settled into her schedule. She helped in the diner until after lunch then worked in her office.

Several times through the week, Noah made an appearance and always took special time out to talk to Sam. He even stood shyly in front of her office door one day to make sure he secured her attention.

On Friday, she went to clean the ten cabins. The rooms on the left side sported a trout theme on one wall. The little cabins on the right were decorated with a woodsy camp theme.

Sam made a list for supplies. She wanted to buy new linens and curtains for the rooms. She also checked the coffee pots to ensure they worked.

In a couple of weeks, the guests would arrive for the season and she wanted to be ready.

While Belle waited on customers, Anne made muffins for the freezer.

Rubbing her hands on her apron, she gave Belle a glance of despair. "I really don't like this. Muffins should be made fresh every morning, not put in the freezer."

Walking past Anne, Belle replied, "I like them. I really can't tell they are frozen."

Anne stopped for a second and laughed. "Yes, I know—that's why I've always done most of the cooking around here." She bagged up the muffins and added, "Don't mind me. I'm old and don't like changes much."

Belle nodded and walked over to help her take the muffins to the freezer. "Anne, things will work out. You'll see."

Sam came in that afternoon and was headed to her office when Noah strolled in. Seeing him, she couldn't stop her smile. "Hi, Noah! How's your day going?"

"I've been busy this morning. I had a mini-mall project over on the north end of town. A Sub King is being built."

Sam couldn't believe how a simple conversation would lift her spirits. "Wow, that's good, isn't it Noah?"

Smiling, Noah agreed. "Yes and some of the locals have plans to open shops. That will help the town. I think we'll even get a Save-U-Bucks store."

Anne looked uneasy. "If you ask me, there are too many changes going on around here."

Turning to Anne, Noah noted the concern in her voice. "I don't know. I think it would be nice not to have to drive out to the interstate to Shopper's Mart every time you need to pick up one or two things."

"Noah, is there something I can get you? Can you stay a bit?"

"Sure Sam, I'll have a cup of coffee and a slice of apple pie."

As Sam walked around the counter, he watched the way her body moved. His eyes drifted to her face and longed to touch the strand of hair that escaped the hair clip she wore.

Clearing his mind, he wondered what was wrong with him. He couldn't remember the last time he let a woman get under his skin this way. Seeing her was the highlight of his day.

Sam broke into Noah's thoughts as she handed him the coffee. "Here Noah, the coffee was just made. Enjoy."

Like a rabbit caught in a trap, he quickly responded, "Yes, I will. Thanks Sam."

As Noah grabbed the coffee cup, he deliberately let his hand rub against Sam's, making her blush.

"Sam, I enjoyed going out with you. Can we do it again sometime?"

Sam's heart thumped in response while she felt heat rise to her cheeks. Shyly, she responded, "Yes, I think I would like that."

That evening, Anne waved goodbye to Belle, and nodded her head toward Sam, offering a slight smile as she walked out the door.

Belle made her way to Sam's office.

"Sam, I think everything is ready for the weekend."

Stopping her work, Sam focused on Belle. She enjoyed seeing the happy spark on the young woman's face. "Thanks and have a good weekend."

Before Belle turned to leave, she eyed Sam. "Are you glad to be here, Sam?"

Pausing, Sam considered her question. "Yes, I am." Shocked at the certainty in her own words, she continued. "I'm surprised that I like this place so much. I never wanted to, but I am more at peace here at the inn than I have been for a long time."

Belle tossed her ponytail aside and added, "I like you, Sam."

Sam closed her ledger and responded back, "I like you too."

With Belle gone, Sam put everything up and turned the door sign over to *Closed*.

Taking in the view from the big front window one last time, Sam's attention wandered toward the parking lot.

She spotted an old model truck sitting across the street, parked on the side of the road close to the trees, as if trying to hide from sight.

An odd feeling she couldn't put her fingers on pricked at Sam, but she shook it off. Anyway, why would she care about an old truck?

Saturday morning came with a bright clear sky. She gazed out the window before she started her day.

One of her favorite past times now was watching nature. She enjoyed the clean crispness of everything. In the distance, the lake sparkled in the sun that reflected off the water, twinkling like miniature lights.

Sam had finally begun to accept deep down in her heart that this was the first time in years she'd been really happy. She was satisfied. Yes, she liked belonging somewhere.

Watching a bird fly over, she wondered how such contentment flourished from living in such a small area. She still wasn't ready to decide what that meant when it came to her future.

Downstairs in the diner, she made the coffee.

The muffins and pie sat under glass and she relaxed at the counter, reading the paper. Sam sensed his presence even before she heard his steps, feeling him in her heart.

Noah walked up to the counter. "Sam, got any blueberry muffins?"

As Sam rose to serve Noah a muffin and coffee, he asked, "Sam will you come and sit with me for a while?"

"Sure."

"Do think you'll be okay here on Saturdays? I mean, things will get busier during the tourist season when the fishing is good."

She sat down at the counter as she answered his question. "I think I'll be okay."

Noah inhaled the fragrance of lilac, enjoying the flowery smell as the fragrance wrapped around his nostrils. "Sam, you sure smell good. What are you doing later?"

As they looked into each other's eyes, she answered, "I thought I'd ride around the lake. I wanted to familiarize myself with the place. That way when the guests arrive, I'll know the area a bit."

Noah listened then moved closer. "I can pick you up and show you around. You know I'm a wealth of information, Sam."

Sam smiled as she remembered the history lesson Noah had given her—and the kiss later.

A spark of anticipation ignited. "That would be nice. You can show me where the best fishing is."

After Noah left, Sam hummed a little song as she worked, already thinking about what the evening had to offer.

Later, she closed the inn and headed upstairs to change. All day she had thought of nothing but this evening and Noah.

A short while later, he rang her doorbell.

Sam couldn't help but stare at Noah's firm frame and think how handsome he was in his faded jeans.

Riding around the lake, Sam studied the size of the reservoir. The trees seemed to stand in just the right places, the tall grasses dancing in the breeze. She could imagine how someone might enjoy an evening basking in all the scenery.

They talked a lot about the fishing at the lake as he drove. While Sam inspected the area, her heart soaked in an inner acceptance—yes, this was certainly a beginning for her. Not the one she had envisioned, but just maybe the start she was supposed to make. She was truly accepting that she had indeed found something she'd missed all these years. Who would have thought it would be in a small town?

Noah parked and they walked around the lake while he pointed out the various places popular with the fishers.

Sam was so relaxed she couldn't believe she would ever get enough of the peaceful countryside. The trees were budding and the birds had started building nests.

She knew this was what her life needed—moving to the county was something she should have done long ago, if only she would have taken the chance before now.

Noah sat on a blanket beside her and reached for her hand. "Do you fish, Sam?"

Sam laughed as an easy feeling settled over her. "I never had anyone take me fishing."

Noah looked across the lake and shook his head. "That's not right, Sam. You need to know how to fish. You can't live on a lake without being an experienced fisherman. I'll teach you how."

She shifted her vision to Noah. "I don't know about becoming experienced, but I just might take you up on that. First though, let me get use to running the inn during the summer."

Excited about teaching Sam, Noah said, "Okay, I have an extra fishing rod that will work great for you to use."

Heading home much later, she hated to see the night end. "Noah, would you like to come up to the apartment for a cup of coffee?"

Noah took a second before he responded. "Are you sure, Sam? I mean yes. I'd like to. If you're sure."

Sam had never encountered a reaction like that from a man before. She sat beside him in disbelief, then quietly added, "I wanted to ask you, Noah. Otherwise, I wouldn't have."

Inside her apartment, Noah noticed the place was different. Sam had added some new pieces of furniture.

Pictures of landscapes and flowers now hung on the walls and the furnishings had been rearranged. The apartment now had a feminine touch.

Sam watched Noah as he glanced around the room and wondered what he was thinking. "Do you like it?"

"Sure. You made a cozy place here, Sam."

He walked around the living room. "I remember when Bo was in the hospital. He asked me to make sure things were taken care of. I told him not to talk like that, but he said he knew his time had come. He wanted me to see that things got done."

Sam saw the shift of Noah's expression as sadness washed over his face. "So what did he want you to do?"

Noah shifted back to the present. "He wanted me to clean out this apartment and give most of his things to a charity. All except for a few things, which he designated for certain people to have. He even made me promise to paint the furniture in the spare bedroom—why, I couldn't figure out."

Startled at that comment, Sam turned her head quickly. "You mean the bedroom with the small fireplace."

"Yes, that's the one. He said he wanted the furniture painted white and the fireplace cleaned out."

The strangest sensation washed over her. "Noah, that's the bedroom I decided to take when I arrived here. I remember the first time I stood in that room. It was like all my troubles just floated away."

Noah smiled. "I guess Bo knew you would like that room then. I often wondered why he had me paint the furniture."

Sam handed Noah a cup and they sat down on the big padded sofa. Noah moved close to Sam and put his arm over the back of the blue couch.

Sam deliberately slowed her breathing, determined to squash the bouncing balls in her stomach. Silently, she wondered why a grown woman would act like this.

She had gone out with men, been deeply involved with them also, so why did she feel like a teenager still in high school?

The warm softness of her leg against his made Noah itch to grab her in a passionate embrace. He fought against his body as he slid his leg farther away and tried to squelch the raw desire that bubbled inside him.

Sam was a hard woman for any man not to want.

Noah pulled Sam close and kissed her. His mouth traveled from her lips to her neck.

Sam's lips searched out Noah's as her heart hammered. She couldn't remember the last time she kissed someone and experienced such longing.

As the night drifted on, they cuddled on the couch and savored each other kisses.

Before he left, he rubbed Sam's shoulder and threw her a question she wasn't ready for and probably never would have been. "Sam, would you go to church with me in the morning?"

Taken aback, she struggled for an answer.

She was determined not to look into those large brown eyes of his for fear she'd say anything just to see his smile light his face up. The words stuck in her throat.

"Noah, I'm not sure I want to. I haven't been to church since I was a child. I remember going a few times, but I just felt so out of place, like I really didn't belong there."

Noah's fingers cupped her chin, tilting her head back slightly. Gently, he turned her to face him. With a kind expression in his voice, he added, "It's just a morning service, Sam. Give it a try."

She perched on the edge of her seat, fighting her emotions. Her butterflies had suddenly turned into a grumbling lion.

Part of her wanted to see what church was all about now that she was grown.

Still, the bigger part of her knew that God didn't have time for the likes of her. Hadn't he already shown her in the past that He had better things to do than shine blessings on her? If He cared, she would have had a lot easier of a life.

Then a nibble of something Bo had said to her once floated in her head.

"Noah, sometimes I think about some of the things Bo shared with me. He talked about Jesus and His grace. I've even read a little of Bible since I moved here. I just don't think I'm ready to go to worship yet."

Noah wrapped his masculine hand around Sam's slender palm. "Sam, I am not asking for you to change your heart about things, just go with me sometime and see for yourself."

She watched Noah's hand on hers. "Uh, can I think about it?"

Noah squeezed her hand and sent Sam a smile that radiated his entire face. "Yes, of course you can. Church and Jesus will always be waiting for you, Sam. Always."

Sam walked Noah to the door. She stood at the entrance and soaked in his embrace as he held her.

She fought the raw emotions that surged through her as Noah's arms wrapped her tight. The explosion of their lips together flared desire in her and Noah's question about church faded away.

Stepping back to gain her composure, Sam searched Noah's face. "Thanks for the evening."

As Noah walked down the apartment steps to his truck, Sam's hand automatically went to the spot on her lips that still throbbed with desire. She watched Noah as he closed the door to his vehicle.

Just as she began to shut her front door, she glanced at the stars, then toward the end of the road.

Did she just see that older model truck travel by at a snail's pace?

Maybe not, but the vehicle seemed to be hanging around the inn a lot.

Sam made her way to her bedroom and wondered about the old vehicle. She was certain whoever owned the truck didn't live below the inn because the lake ended there.

So far, the few houses she'd noticed on the road didn't seem to own any vehicles that dated. She certainly had never noticed the truck parked in their driveways.

The next day, Sam dawdled in bed a little longer than usual. She watched the fire in the fireplace while her thinking centered on Noah.

Sam could still taste his lips on hers. She closed her eyes, remembering the passion that sparked between them.

She contemplated Noah and her life now in Big Fork Lake, Alabama. She questioned if she could live in this small town all her life. Would she be happy? Or would she grow to miss the city?

Then, lying there staring at the ceiling, her attention moved to Jesus.

How could anyone have a *personal* connection with the Lord? The idea seemed so impossible to her, the thought of God so vast and impossible. And yet Bo and Noah...they both acted as if Jesus were their best friend. Was she missing something they'd found?

All those questions occurred to her and more as she sat up and fluffed her pillow a little too hard. Man oh man. How could a simple kiss from a handsome man have messed with her head so bad? Have her questioning everything in life?

Sam turned her head and picked up the Bible she'd placed on the nightstand. Cautiously, she opened to the bookmark. She didn't understand what all of the Psalms were about, but the words were comforting.

Her hand encountered the rough texture of the leather, her very own Bible, the one she had found in the dresser drawer of her new bedroom.

Sam traveled back to a few days after she arrived there. She was putting up her things and feeling grateful that Bo had been in her life.

That was when she came across the Bible.

When she flipped the pages of the white book, she spotted Bo's handwriting. *Sam, open your heart to Jesus, your forever friend, Bo.*

CHAPTER SIX

The weeks came and went and everyone seemed to adjust to the way things had changed around the inn.

Noah stopped by several afternoons right when Sam was getting ready to close and they spent time together over a dessert. They sat together and held each other.

On most Saturdays, they went to Big Fork Fish Camp together. When they kissed, Sam knew desire sparked in him.

No doubt, Noah wanted more, but he never attempted to go beyond kissing and cuddling her.

Indeed, Noah was a hard man to understand.

The evening before the fishing season officially kicked off several guests had already checked into the cabins.

Sam was surprised at the inner tranquility in her life now. All thoughts of leaving Big Fork Lake had vanished. She didn't even question her decision anymore. Now that she had grown used to the inn, it fit her like a glove.

Once she'd checked in her new guests, Noah invited Sam to explore the lake. Her mind wandered as she rode beside Noah. Two months had passed since she arrived here in this town. She couldn't be happier.

They walked and held hands then finally settled down on a blanket to enjoy a picnic. Sam basked in the peaceful evening, relishing the slower pace that'd become her life.

She and Noah seemed to be growing closer, but she couldn't help but wonder what direction their lives were headed.

Sam had come to realize that she wanted Noah in her life, even if the man was a Christian. She knew though that his belief wasn't something he'd ever relinquish, nor would he ever stop trying to save her.

Inwardly smiling, she compared him to Bo.

Just as Bo had done, Noah would gently bring up scriptures or something about Jesus from time to time. He didn't pressure her, but nor did he ignore the topic.

She listened to the birds twittering as she stretched out her legs. Glancing at the trees, she followed the path of shade that the leaves were now starting to create and noticed a few fishing boats in the distance.

As they sat on the blanket, Noah pondered the bond he and Sam were forming. He mulled over the talks he'd had with God, asking for help to find someone special. Was this her? How could it be her if she didn't believe? Had He put her in his life to help Sam see God's mercy and grace?

Sam looked over at Noah and a rush of giddiness she couldn't explain swept through her. "Noah, what are you thinking?"

Noah picked up Sam's hand from the blanket and kissed her fingers. "I was thinking about you." His face grew serious. "Sam, I need to say something to you."

An air of uncertainty surrounded Sam. Her smile faded, not understanding why he appeared so solemn. Her thoughts shifted. Something must be wrong. Was this the old kiss-off?

Noah scrutinized Sam and inhaled a long breath, not sure how to explain what he wanted to share with her, but he needing to express what was on his mind if there was ever going to be anything permanent between them.

"Sam, we've gotten close these past few months. I care for you very much. I have prayed for someone in my life that I can have a relationship with. But I don't really know how you feel about me."

Sam wanted him, but wasn't sure she knew how to respond. Indeed, she'd never known anyone like Noah.

Sam certainly couldn't remember any man ever *asking* her when he wanted to get serious.

"Noah, I do care about you. I've never enjoyed being with anyone as much as I do you. I want very much for us to get closer."

Noah stretched out on the blanket, silently asking God to give him the words to say.

He knew he had to explain. Deep down, he was starting to believe he and Sam were supposed to be together.

"There is something I need you to understand. I am a Christian and I have lived for the Lord a long time. Not just in words, but in my actions. Separating myself from worldly things is hard sometimes. I just try to keep my faith." Noah fondled her hand as he continued, "Sam, do you feel that we can have something permanent one day?"

Her expression questioned him. "Noah, you've never hidden the fact that the Lord is part of your life. I've never been romantically involved with any one religious before, but I am willing to give it a try."

She wondered where this conversation was headed. So what if Noah was a Christian? What did that really mean anyway?

Noah watched Sam with uncertainty, hoping she understood. Anyway, he knew that if their relationship was right, then things would work out.

Sam wiggled on the blanket, her attention toward the lake as she tried to digest all Noah had shared. The word permanent ping-ponged around in her head. Sam had always understood Noah was a man who believed in God, but she didn't know exactly what his faith had to do with them being together.

For the first time her feelings about Noah made her a little uncomfortable.

"It's been a long time since I've enjoyed being with someone as much as I do you. For the first time in years, I have the notion that maybe I wasn't meant to be alone."

Noah scooted closer to Sam and with caution in his voice responded, "Sam when I become seriously involved with someone, I want the person to be someone God has chosen for me and it will be forever.

"I think God used Bo to lead you here. This is difficult for me. I want you, but you need to understand the way I live my life."

Noah scooted closer to Sam and searched her face.

"Sam, I will never push you into anything. If you ever want to learn more about God, I think that's great. If you don't, then we will work that out also. The Lord guides us—sometimes our time is just not His. I need to make sure you understand why our relationship is different."

Sam was still struggling to figure out exactly what all that meant. "Noah, I really don't know what to say, but I am sure I want to be with you." She smiled at Noah, taking in the warmth of his arm around her shoulders. "I've come to think that maybe my situation would be better if one day I could trust in God. I'm just slow at making decisions. I guess I don't understand myself at times. What direction I'm going in."

Noah's laugh rang out in amusement as he hugged her. "Sam, the Lord will guide us. You'll see...we'll just leave things the way they are for now. If you ever decide you want to learn more about the Lord, your first step is to go to church with me."

The next week was a busy at the inn. The rooms had been refreshed with new linens and curtains and Sam had checked in five guests so far. The season had started out well.

Every morning, guests strolled in for coffee and the biscuits Sam had added to the menu.

Anne didn't take much to the frozen bread, even if she did agree they saved time.

June came and Sam totally accepted that she wanted the inn as her home forever. That night, as Sam and Noah dined at Big Fork Fish Camp, Sam made it known to Noah that she was going to church with him Sunday.

"Are you sure, Sam? I don't want you to feel like you're being pushed—that's why I haven't said any more on the subject."

Sam snickered as she watched the funny expression on his face. His demeanor reminded her of a child at Christmas time.

"Noah, yes I'm sure. I've been reading my Bible and have learned that you don't have to be perfect for the Lord to accept you. Since I moved to Big Fork Lake, a lot of the ways that I see things have changed."

Taking a bite of fish, Noah said, "I'll pick you up at ten o'clock in the morning so we can ride together."

Later that night, at Sam's door, Noah kissed her goodnight.

His broad chest pressed against hers, molding their desires. A desperate longing saturated her body like nothing she'd known before.

As Noah left, Sam shut the door on her longing, paying no heed to the older model truck that positioned itself across the street, discreetly placed in the shadows the moonlight cast.

Lying in bed, Sam adjusted her pillow and scanned through the past months, thinking about Big Fork Lake.

She now believed wholeheartedly this was where she belonged, but also wondered if God led her to this place for another reason.

Even if nothing else happened between her and Noah, she accepted the fact that God should be in her life. Just how did she make the move toward His grace? She really didn't know yet. She realized now that God was there for her and had been all along, but she was too stuck on blaming him for everything bad that happened to see the truth.

Turning off her lamp, she thought about a verse in the Bible. Finally, she understood what Bo meant by some of the things he said. God's word did make more sense to her now. Turning over, she grinned. Of course she understood the Bible more—listening to Noah had certainly opened her eyes to many things.

Monday morning, Belle walked in the diner with her face beaming as she searched out Sam. "Sam, it was good to see you in church with Noah yesterday."

Setting out the muffins for the day, Sam remarked contently, "Yes, church was nice. Pastor Stevens is a good person. I like living here, so I want to be a part of this place."

Belle flashed Sam a big grin. "That's good Sam. I hoped you'd stick around."

Anne slipped out from the kitchen, hearing part of their conversation. "Things are pretty cozy between you two, huh? Even going to church together. I hope things work out."

Belle's gaze passed from one woman to the other. "What are you two talking about?"

Anne's face brightened and she smiled. "Oh, Sam has been going out with Noah *a lot* lately."

Sam shot Anne a quick look. "How did you know that?"

Anne moved over and poured a cup of coffee. "You know this is a little town. Things get around."

Patting Sam on the arm, Anne commented, "You've made this your home now or so it seems."

As the sheriff walked in, he heard the last comment. "Are you here to stay?"

In a flash, Sam decided she would fess up to the decision she'd made about the town. "I *am* here to stay. This is what Bo wanted and now I know it's what I want."

Sheriff Gruver searched the women's faces without commenting on Sam's remark. "Belle, I need coffee and a biscuit to go."

On the way out the door, the sheriff tipped his head at Sam.

Sam gestured in his direction. She noticed a slight turn of his lips, making his stern face appear softer.

That short conversation fueled Sam, making her think about things in her life. She wasn't sure about Noah, but she did enjoy going to church, and was beginning to understand she could be a child of God.

On the following Friday morning, Noah stopped by for his usual cup of coffee. "Hi Sam." He playfully tucked Sam's hair behind her ear. "Once you've finished your day tomorrow, how about we catch a movie?"

Elated, she responded, "I haven't been to a movie in forever. I think that would be fun."

As Noah turned to leave, he walked to Sam and kissed her lightly.

Sam turned around to see Belle's approving smile as she strolled past into the kitchen.

At six o'clock the following evening, Noah stood at her door and knocked. He'd been counting down the hours until he could see Sam.

He'd rifled through his past, trying to remember when a woman had ever made him feel the way Sam did. The one woman years ago who he had loved—and thought loved him—certainly didn't cause the stir of emotions that Sam created.

All he hoped was that Sam understood where he came from and could accept that his being a Christian kept him from acting on his fleshly desires. As hard as that was to control at times.

Opening her door, Sam carried a huge smile across her face. After a long kiss, Noah escorted Sam to his truck.

On the way to the mall, they talked about the fishing season and the inn. Noah told her about his week. Then he said, "Sam, I've missed you."

Inwardly she smiled. "Missed me? You've stopped by to see me just about every other evening."

Noah took her hand in his. "I know, but I haven't had much time alone with you these past two weeks."

Sam laid her hand on his and enjoyed the sense of belonging that she experienced every time she was with him. "I know. I'm sorry I had to call off last Friday."

Noah gave her a huge smile. "It's okay. Things got busy at the inn sometimes for Bo also. Bo wasn't as picky as you are though."

Sam's voice rose in a teasing sound. "What do you mean by that, Noah Frye?"

Shyly, Noah glanced over at Sam. "I just don't like it when we can't see each other."

Once at the mall, they went to eat at a Mexican restaurant before they settled in at the theater.

Sam seated herself beside Noah, enjoying the movie. She delighted in the comfort of being in a dark theater beside him. As they sat there and held hands, sharing popcorn and laughing at the comedy, she breathed contentedly. How lucky she was to have found Big Fork Lake.

After the movie, Sam and Noah strolled past storefronts at the mall. "I really liked the movie, Noah. Thanks for bringing me."

Noah held her hand tighter. "I enjoyed the movie. I feel like a teenager tonight."

Sam giggled at that comment. "Do you think that's a good thing, Noah?"

He matched his steps with hers as he said, "I think so, at least for a little while."

On the drive back to Sam's apartment, Sam rested her head on Noah's shoulder. Quietly, she wished she could stay that way until morning.

Unfortunately, Noah pulled into the parking lot at the inn in what seemed the blink of an eye. "Here you are Sam, home way too fast."

His kisses sent Sam's heart into a whirl—she wanted his lips on hers all night, but the day had been busy and she was exhausted.

Forcing restraint, she lifted her head and deeply stared into his eyes, gazing into the raw passion that simmered.

She hated to move, but pushed back a little anyway. "Noah, I would ask you in, but it's really late."

Noah slowly released Sam and leaned his forehead on hers as their eyes met. "I know. Like I said, I feel like a teenager."

Not understanding, Sam shook her head. "What do you mean?"

Noah spoke while he traced small circles on her lips. "When I was young, I had to go straight home too."

Sam couldn't help but burst out with laughter. "Aw Noah, I will make this up to you."

Sam threw her arms around Noah for one last kiss and locked her lips to his in a raw, passionate display of lust that she was sure he would remember.

Noah forgot to breathe, thinking only of the kiss. He watched as Sam walked up her living quarters.

During the short drive home, he pictured her in his arms. In one heated moment, he gave into his fantasy. Quickly he turned his truck around and headed back to the inn, to Sam, to face down his desires.

As he approached, his eyes cut to an older model truck sitting at the end of the drive that led to the inn.

Gradually, he slowed down. Noah spotted a shadow in Sam's window. It appeared to be two figures standing close together and moving in unison.

He watched intently from his truck and raised his voice sharply in the air. "What? So this is the real reason she didn't want me to come up tonight? She has someone else. Lord, I am such a fool."

An upsurge of heat crawled through his body as anger took hold. Noah hit the steering wheel and ground his teeth to keep from releasing the various curses he wanted to spew.

He fought to stay in control, knowing that if he gave in and blurted his verbal frustrations, he'd just have to ask forgiveness for his foul mouth.

Turning around, he spun gravel in the aftermath of his truck tires.

The next morning, Sam waited for Noah to pick her up. She noticed the time was ten-fifteen—usually Noah showed by now. Finally, after ten more minutes, she hopped in her car and headed to church.

At church, Sam finally spotted Noah. She waved to get his attention, but he turned his head and deliberately avoided her.

To Sam's surprise, he chose to take a seat in the back where only enough room remained in the pew for one more amongst the crowd of mothers with young children.

During the service, Sam tried hard to keep her mind on the truth Pastor Stevens relayed, but all she could think about was finding out what was up with Noah.

Every time she turned her head his way, he made a point to read his Bible.

The last call for prayer was issued and the church let out. Sam hurried to catch Noah as he rushed across the parking lot in long strides.

"Noah, what's wrong? Noah!"

After he didn't respond, Sam became irritated and raised her voice. "Noah, where were you this morning? What's going on?"

Noah stopped abruptly and looked sternly at Sam. Never had she seen such fury shining in his eyes.

Noah glared at her as he muttered, "You really have to ask, Sam?"

She stood there clueless. Questions raced around in her mind as she searched Noah's face.

Several members of the church passed by, saying their goodbyes as Noah's eyes pierced the short distance between them.

He stuffed his hands in his pockets. "Sam, I certainly don't want to have words here at church in front of everyone."

Sam was at a loss. "But Noah, what's wrong with you?"

He glared at Sam. In a calculated declaration, he issued, "I don't think the town needs to know our business, Sam." Noah turned to get in his truck.

Not knowing what else to do, Sam spoke up curtly, her voice revealing the irritation she felt. "Noah, right now! I want you to tell me what's wrong! I'll wait in my car until everyone has left, but we need to talk."

Noah shrugged his shoulders. "Suit yourself, Sam. I'm going up the street to buy a cola."

Sam cringed at his remark and marched to his truck door, forcing her will. "Noah, I demand to talk today, right here."

Noah watched the yard beyond her and drew a hard breath. "Yeah, I know. I'll be back."

While Sam sat in her car, she wondered what in the world was going on. She blew out heated sounds and tapped her foot in aggravation.

For the next twenty minutes, she punched in stations on her radio. Her emotions fumed with anger and she was glad she hadn't told him how she really felt about him.

Eventually, he returned. Sam stepped out and went over to his truck. Noah rolled down his window and coldly ordered Sam to get in.

As she shut the door, she snapped, "Noah. What is up with you?"

Noah focused on the trees outside his truck window. "Oh, that is really funny, Sam." Turning slightly, Noah spoke between gritted teeth as he toyed with his cola bottle. "I won't play this game. I know about everything."

With a slight turn of his head, he spat out, "Last night, I wanted so much to spend more time with you."

Sam didn't understand what he meant, so she rushed in, "Okay Noah, I'm sorry I sent you away but—"

His irritated voice interrupted what Sam was going to say next. "Let me speak. I left your place last night and when I got into town, I turned around and came back to the inn. When I got there, I saw you two."

When Noah didn't say anything else, she spoke up. "What are you talking about?"

He blew a breath, forcing control he didn't feel. "I saw the truck, Sam. I think I've seen the old thing around before, but I never thought much about it. I've been so stupid. I will not be used."

Sam straightened and hugged close to the side of the door. "Noah, I still don't understand what you are talking about."

He gave her a quick sneer and continued. "Sam, I won't be involved with you when you can't be faithful. I should have expected this. I thought you understood me."

Sam still couldn't figure out what he was getting at, but behind the fury, she saw genuine pain in Noah's eyes.

Slowly she said, "Noah, I enjoy being with you. I'm fine with our relationship. I don't understand what you are implying."

Jerking his head, he glared fiercely at her. "You *know* what I'm talking about. That truck parked at the end of your driveway and way past one in the morning. I'm no dummy—there's only one reason why a vehicle would be there. We both know that."

"Noah, I don't know anything about that old truck."

He gripped the steering wheel and twisted his hand around the circle. "I'm very aware that you're a beautiful woman. I know I haven't shown you how desirable you are."

Now realization smacked her in the face. She was shocked that Noah thought she had been seeing someone else. "Noah, there is no one in my life except you!"

The hurt threatened to cut off her air and she willed herself not to show any emotion. "You're the only man I've gone out with since I arrived here."

He clenched his lips together and then blurted, "Yeah right, you two must spend some cozy nights laughing at the old country boy."

Sam looked at Noah with bewilderment and forced the tears to stay buried. "Noah, you are the only man I'm seeing, but I have noticed that truck before."

Noah lowered his voice, showing no mercy. "Sam, will you just go? Get out of my truck."

Too shocked to respond, she opened the truck door and slid out of the vehicle.

The following two weeks trudged by and Sam stayed busy with the inn. Things were busy for the season and she was doing a decent job at keeping her mind off Noah.

That Friday, Belle asked about Noah. "Sam, I haven't seen Noah around lately. What's going on?"

Sam had tried, but she could not hide her heartache, not from Belle. "Oh, we had a disagreement...or I should say he misunderstood something. For some reason, Noah convinced himself I have another man in my life."

Belle wrinkled up her face as she threw Sam a shocked look. "But you don't."

Sam's heart tore as she concentrated on the floor. "I know that, but I couldn't get Noah to see the truth."

Belle lightly rested her hand on Sam's shoulder and offered half a smile. "Sam, I'm sorry. Maybe he will change his mind."

When Sam walked off to hide into her office, she did not hear Anne speak to Belle. "What was that? Sam and Noah broke up?"

Belle shook her head. "Yes, Anne, I think they have."

Picking up a towel, Anne spoke frankly. "Maybe it's for the best."

Belle glanced at Anne in amazement. "Anne, what do you mean?"

"Sam's a nice woman. I just don't know if she fits in with Noah. She's only been here a few months."

Belle couldn't identify with Anne's reasoning. "Sometimes you're a little funny toward Sam."

Nonchalantly, Anne shrugged. "You know me, I see things in a different way. Sam's okay."

That evening as Sam said goodbye to the ladies, Anne showed concern for Sam. "Sam, I'm sorry to hear you're having trouble with Noah. What happened?"

Sam responded, even though all she wanted was to forget. "Oh Anne, I really don't want to talk about Noah right now. He just decided I was someone he couldn't trust."

Anne smiled kindly toward Sam. "You know, Sam, sometimes things don't work out the way we think they should, but it's for the best. You'll be all right."

Thirty minutes later, Sam hung the close sign in the window and trudged up the steps to her apartment.

Sam lay in her tub. Thoughts of Noah rushed into her mind.

No, she would not give into tears. That was over. She'd cried on the way home that day. She was determined not to cry anymore. Even though her heart would hurt for a while, she would get over this.

Scrubbing her face vigorously, his words played in her mind. But she had done just fine without him before and she would move on and make a good life for herself. After all, she didn't need him to be happy.

Sam couldn't help a surge of regret. If only she knew why this had happened. What caused him to come to such a conclusion? Thank goodness, she still had the inn to keep her busy.

Sam skipped down the stairs. Three weeks had come and gone since she saw Noah. She still experienced a twinge of hurt every so often when she thought of him, but she remained strong. Her days stayed busy keeping the inn going.

She had all but two vacancies occupied and the end of June didn't show any sign of slowing. Everyone seemed to accept her as the new owner and she was proud of the job did.

The weather turned unbearably hot, so Sam scheduled service on all the air conditioner units in the rooms. That day, Sam stayed busy with deliveries and had to escort the service technician to the different cabins.

She finally made her way to the bank at the last minute. Sam walked back in the inn as Anne finished talking to a couple who planned to stay a week.

Looking up at Sam, Anne furrowed her brow with concern. "You're tired, Sam."

Sam blew a piece of her hair out of her eye. "Yes Anne, I am. This has been a busy day."

Anne moved her head in agreement. "Let me fix you a glass of tea and you go on up to your apartment and relax."

Glancing at her wristwatch, she noticed the time. "Are you sure, Anne?"

Watching Sam slump on the stool, Anne nodded a resounding yes.

"You've run back and forth all day. I'll lock up this evening."

Anne disappeared into the kitchen to fix Sam a glass of tea and the door chimed. A middle-age man carrying fishing poles strolled in.

Seeing Sam, he announced, "I have a reservation. I'm James Brookshire."

Sam perked with one last burst of energy and walked over to the end of the counter to the guestbook while the man scanned the painting on the wall.

"So, how is the fishing?"

Sam recalled what someone said earlier that day and replied, "Great—at least, that's what everyone has told me."

The man handed her his credit card. "Good. I need a few days of just the fish and me."

The man glanced on the counter at the pastries and pies. "Maybe I will come back after I unpack to get some of that dessert."

Sam smiled and looked in the direction of the tray. "I have some very good blueberry pie."

Anne came out of the kitchen and handed Sam a glass of tea. "Here Sam, I'll finish checking him in. You take this tea and go up to your apartment and rest."

Sam flashed the guest a big grin as she started toward the stairs. "Thanks, Anne. It's nice to meet you, Mr. Brookshire."

When she arrived upstairs to her apartment, she kicked off her shoes and staggered a little as she made her way to her bedroom. The heat had really gotten to her.

Sitting on the side of her bed, she sipped the last of her tea. She was glad she had the air conditioners serviced. The weatherman called for some simmering weeks ahead.

As Sam rested on the edge of her bed, she took the clip out of her hair and swayed from side to side.

She knew she was overtired. She had trouble just keeping her eyes open. Sluggishly, Sam placed her empty glass down on her bedside table and slipped under the sheet, enjoying the cool feel of the cotton material.

The last thing that came to mind before she drifted off was that she needed to sleep for a couple of hours. Then she would feel better.

The next morning was the annual fishing tournament at Big Fork Lake. Anne and Belle were busy serving guests coffee.

Anne looked at Belle with concern. "Wonder why Sam isn't down here helping?"

Belle took a side-glance toward the steps that led to her apartment. "I don't know. She's always helped when we're busy."

Sam rushed out of the shower and fussed at herself.

She'd never slept late since arriving in Big Fork Lake—she had always gotten up early.

Sam mentally counted the time she had been in Big Fork Lake—five months without any regrets. Then the memory of Noah clouded her mind. She pushed the thought aside. At least she didn't have any bad qualms about being here at the inn.

Rushing down the stairs, she faced the day. "Hi Anne, Belle. I'm sorry I am late."

Belle's wide smile outlined her perky face. "That's okay, Sam."

Anne walked out of the kitchen and spotted Sam. "Are you okay this morning, Sam?"

"Yeah, Anne, I just overslept."

Settling down from the rush of the morning, Sam headed out to clean the cabins. A few hours into her routine, Sam hurried back to the diner to take a break.

Belle paused from cleaning a table and grinned. "I'll get you something cold to drink, Sam. You sit down."

Coming over to the booth, Belle sat down across from Sam as she handed her a glass. "Hey, I know it's none of my business, but why not call Noah? I know you miss him."

Sam eyed her and took an exasperated breath. "He made things clear. He doesn't want to see me. Besides, he knows where I am."

Belle picked at a napkin and crushed the paper in her hand as she spoke. "Why does he think you're seeing someone else?"

Sam hesitated then glanced around the room. All but one customers had left and Anne was in the kitchen. "Because of the truck, Belle."

An odd expression crossed Belle's face. "What truck are you talking about?"

Relief washed over Sam and made her realize she wanted to talk about the misunderstanding. "I haven't said anything, but ever since I've been here, I've been seeing an older model, dark color truck hanging around. Sometimes I notice it parked across the street.

"Late at night, the truck often drives by the inn several times, always in the dark. But I really hadn't thought much about it."

"Noah and I went to the movies a few weeks ago. After he left my apartment, he turned around and came back this way, and saw that old truck parked at the end of the lot. That was before any of the tourists had checked in, so Noah assumed I had a man here with me.

"Belle, I'm just sick about our breakup. I care a lot about Noah. I really thought he was the one." Wiggling her shoulders, she added, "But things change, so I'll go on, and forget about him."

Belle rubbed her chin. Despite Sam's resolve, she witnessed the sadness that washed over her friend's face. "Sam, I think you should try to talk to him. Tell him what you have told me."

Disheartened, Sam replied, "It won't do any good. I tried. He's already made his mind up."

Sam rose to leave. As she walked toward the door, she turned. "Belle, I'm glad I talked to you. You are a good friend."

Belle looked at Sam, unsure of what to say. "Sam, I'm glad to be your friend."

Sam returned to cleaning the remaining rooms. She liked Belle, but now she wished she hadn't talked to her about Noah. The memories just caused her heart to hurt more.

Once again, the pain surfaced. Now she was going to have to bury it all over again.

Despite that, she was sure in her heart that she was ready to start a new life with the Lord.

Deep inside, she even held out some hope that maybe one day Noah would see the truth. She was mad at him. If only he wasn't so stubborn and would listen.

Sam walked into the cabin with a seven painted on the front. As she went inside, she glanced at the number. She'd always considered seven lucky.

Changing the bed, Sam's spirits lifted. She was determined to stay in a positive mood.

She would make the best of things—after all, she had the inn.

Sam added clean sheets and stored the dirty ones in her pushcart.

Grabbing clean towels, she pushed the dirty linens outside and went back in the room, heading into the bathroom for the soiled towels.

Stumbling over something, she threw out her hand and grabbed the wall to catch her fall.

Scanning the dim room, she hesitated as her eyes fell on a large shape lying still on the floor. Her sight followed the massive lump balled in the doorway.

She realized what she was seeing and screamed. Her hand flew to her throat as she choked back nausea.

She shivered at the sight of a man curled on the floor, his body lay stiff, just inside the entry. In horror, she stared at the guest she'd checked in the day before.

Her teeth bit into her lip as she forced her jittery finger to punch the numbers for help.

"Now Sam, I need you to tell me one more time what happened."

"Sheriff, I've already told you twice."

Sheriff Gruver wrote in his tablet as he shot her a doubtful look. "Things don't add up. You're the only one who goes into the cabins. The place is covered with your fingerprints."

She glanced back at the room with a huff of frustration. "Of course my fingerprints are in the room. I clean all the rooms."

The sheriff reached for his cuffs. "I have no choice but to arrest you, Sam. It appears that man has been poisoned and until the autopsy comes in, I'm considering this a homicide."

Shock registered on her face. "Sheriff, if I did anything wrong why would I call 9-1-1?"

Snapping on the handcuffs, he eyed her. He had never thought much of her. He'd seen women like her before, the kind that found it easy to take advantage of people, but he couldn't help but wonder. Murder didn't fit her somehow.

"I have to take you in, Sam. We'll know more in a couple of hours."

At the sheriff's office, the deputy led her to a cell. She paced the small area and snarled her nose at the awful odor.

Sam surveyed the room in disgust. A thin bunk with a yellowed sheet thrown across the end was only furniture in the small area. How in the world did anyone use the toilet when it sat in the corner without walls? Even the little sink was too ghastly to wash in.

How could anyone possibly sleep in such a horrible place? One would think they would at least keep the room smelling better.

Everything that'd happened raced through her mind while she battled a sick stomach and tried to control her trembling insides.

She looked at the ceiling and tossed questions to God. "Why is this happening, Lord? I thought I was doing right. I believed in you!"

Sam quivered. She was scared and at that point very insecure. She'd never been in jail.

Sheriff Gruver cut into her thoughts as he stepped up to the cell. "Sam, you may as well settle down. You can't walk the floors all night."

Sam tried not to let her fear show on her face. In a voice he could hardly hear, she replied, "I doubt I could even sit still, Sheriff."

Late that evening, Noah's phone rang as he was unlocking his door. Throwing his keys down on the couch, he made his way inside and snatched up the receiver.

One the other end on the line, he listened to the panicked sound of Belle's voice. "Noah, I have to talk to you!"

Noah inhaled a breath, thinking that the only time Belle called his house was when something bad happened. The last reason had been Bo.

A bad taste formed in his mouth. "What's up?

Noah heard her hesitate. "Noah, I'm calling about Sam."

Noah tossed out a huff, letting air escape hard through his nostrils as aggravation threatened to emerge. "I *don't* want to talk to you about Sam. There's nothing you can fix."

Noah listened to a sound that might have been a pen clicking on the other end of the line before she came back with a fast response. "Noah, I don't want to pry. I do know some of what happened but I also know it's none of my business. However, I do want to say something."

He rolled his eyes. He knew she wouldn't let go of this conversation until she had her say. "Okay spit it out. I might have jumped to conclusions, but you haven't been in my shoes. I know what I saw."

She ignored his comment and responded sarcastically, "You *think* you know! *I* know how Sam feels about you, Noah Frye. She does not want another man. Furthermore, I have *never* seen her with anyone else."

Uncertain as to whether he wanted to hear what she had to tell him or hang up, he hesitated. "Yes, well you don't know everything she does, Belle."

But Belle seemed determined to say her piece. "No Noah, I'm sure I don't, but things have a way of getting around in Big Fork Lake. I would have heard something if she had another man."

Noah didn't want to admit that maybe she was right, but that still didn't explain what he saw. "I'm not sure yet, Belle. I have a hard time trusting sometimes."

Belle liked Noah and figured she had said enough, but offered him one last thought. "Yes well, maybe that's something you need to pray about and seek an answer for. Anyway, that isn't why I called, that was just something I had to say."

"Okay, why did you call?"

"Sam is in jail."

"*What?*" Noah shouted into the receiver. "I mean, what did you say?"

Belle smiled, satisfied at the concern in Noah's voice. "Sheriff Gruver arrested her. A man died in room seven." Pausing she added, "Noah, someone murdered him and they took Sam in." Sounding overwhelmed, she continued, "I just thought you might want to know."

Noah pressed his fingers against his temples as a thousand locked-up emotions crawled out. Defeated, he replied, "Yes, thank you for calling me."

Noah slumped down on the couch and covered his face with his hands. Why was this happening? All the old feelings he harbored for Sam flooded in, stirring his emotions into a whirlwind.

He *did* care for her. He wasn't ready yet to examine what that meant, but the last weeks had been hard. He'd had to fight tooth and nail to keep from going over to the inn and taking Sam in his arms. He wanted so much to believe her.

Struggling with mixed emotions, he talked aloud to the Lord. "I just don't understand any of this. This is probably one time I need to take Belle's advice. I do need to pray. First, let me call my uncle. Sam is going to need a lawyer."

The sheriff stomped to Sam's cell and unlocked the door. "Sam, you have a visitor." He escorted her to a small room.

There she faced a tall thin man with white hair, dressed in a tailored suit, and wearing glasses. The man turned to Sam. "Hello, Ms. Blacker. I'm Frank Cane, attorney-at-law. I'm Noah's uncle from Montgomery. Noah called and wanted me to come by and see if I could be of any assistance to you. If you don't need representation, I'll go."

Sam's head lifted, her attention sparked at the mention of Noah. "No, please don't go. You said Noah sent you?"

The tall man glanced down at Sam and slightly smiled. "Yes, he called me last night. He said to tell you he was praying about things."

Hearing Noah's name stabbed Sam's heart, but she was certainly grateful he'd sent someone who could help her.

"Thank you for coming, Mr. Cane. I didn't murder anyone. I didn't even know the man. Can you help me?"

The long-framed lawyer pulled up a chair and took out his notebook. "Let's start by you telling me what happened, Ms. Blacker."

Putting her elbows on the table, she started to recount the details. "I always do the cleaning in the cabins on Friday. When I walked into room seven, I first changed the bed. Then I push the cart with the dirty sheets outside.

"When I went back into the room and started into the bathroom, I stumbled over the man who'd checked in the evening before—Mr. Brookshire. He was lying on the floor, so I called 9-1-1."

He glanced over a report he'd placed in his composition book. "Sheriff Gruver said the man had eaten a slice of pie that contained enough berries containing poison seeds to kill him."

Sam bit her lip as she recalled what the sheriff had informed her of early that morning. "Yes, I know. That's what he told me. I don't know anything about any berries. I ordered some blueberry pies from a warehouse in Montgomery."

Straightening in the chair, Mr. Cane responded, "Ms. Blacker, they couldn't find any pies or invoice from an order. That points suspicion to you."

Sam pushed up and stood at the table. Her insides rolled from the cold egg she had for breakfast. All she wanted at this point was to get out of this awful place, retreat to her peaceful bedroom and collapse.

"Mr. Cane, the invoice has to be there. I laid it in my office and I stacked those pies in the freezer myself."

Mr. Cane rose from his seat. "I can't do anything until Monday, Ms. Blacker, when the judge will give you a bail hearing."

Monday. It couldn't come soon enough, but at least she wouldn't be stuck in this miserable cell forever. Sam smiled, blowing out in relief. "Thank you, Mr. Cane. I just want to get out of jail."

Frank Cane extended his hand and tried to reassure her. "I'll do what I can. I don't make any promises, Ms. Blacker."

Relief soared through Sam. She knew in her heart he would try to get her free. As he started to turn for the door, she called after him, "Mr. Cane, will you please call me Sam?"

Turning his head, he offered her a sympathetic smile. "I will speak with you the first part of the week, after I contact the judge."

By Sunday morning, Sam's head was spinning. Her nerves sloshed about like a bucket of water. Worry had eaten at her all during the night. Pacing the cell, she recalled an old saying of her grandmother's. She had to agree. She did feel rough as a corncob today.

Stuck between a rock and hard place, Sam decided the only thing left to do was ask the Lord to help her. Maybe He would, maybe He wouldn't. She remembered her troubles in Atlanta and started to lose her bravery as fear rose again like vile in her throat—except this time, she faced prison.

Later that afternoon, she received another visitor. "Are you okay, Sam?"

As Sam perched on the edge of the old wooden chair, she soaked in his brown eyes and unruly hair and searched his face for anything that would relay what he was thinking.

Her heart swelled at the sound of his deep voice.

As she sat there, her emotions swayed back and forth. After all, she didn't do any wrong, but he certainly wouldn't listen to her. Why did she even care if he was here to see her?

As those thoughts stampeded her mind, her heart turned against her. The relief of seeing his face was all that mattered.

"Noah, I'm glad you came by. Thank God you sent Mr. Cane. I was so upset and I didn't know what to do. How did you find out?"

Noah stared into her big blue eyes, his heart swelling with anticipation. He had prayed before he went to bed last night with an open heart, listening to hear what God would lead him to do.

Sunday morning he woke and after talking to Pastor Stevens, he was sure God wanted him to be with Sam.

"Belle called to tell me. She was persistent and started me thinking about the things I said. I've done a lot of talking to the Lord."

The sorrow on his face tested her heart.

"Sam, I need to apologize to you. I jumped to conclusions. I care about you very much and at the time, I worried you wanted more than I could give you."

Sam examined the heartbreaking despair that shined in Noah's eyes. Gauging his expression, she wavered between giving into her heart and obeying her pride.

She knew she ought to be hard to convince, not so easy to win over, but if she was truthful about it, she just wanted Noah back. The rest she would sort out in time. They could talk later.

"Noah, I care about you too. I never wanted to see anyone else. I know I should have told you about that vehicle. But I told myself it was nothing."

"You should have told me? What are you talking about Sam?"

Sam hung her head, regretting that she hadn't mentioned anything about that old vehicle. "That truck you saw. I've seen that old truck hanging around for months. Most of the time it's parked across the street, but some nights the truck passes by the inn several times after dark."

Noah couldn't believe what he heard. He watched her intently, taking a moment to digest what she said. Did she fathom at all what she was telling him? "Sam, you shouldn't have kept this from me."

"I thought if I said something, I'd be making a fuss over nothing. This is a small town—things are different, not like the city."

Deflated, he spoke slowly. "Sam, having someone who sits in a vehicle watching you is not normal no matter where you live. You can't keep things like this from me. I am here for you and you need to tell me about situations that bother you."

Sam closed her eyes and shook her head. "Yes, I realize that now, Noah. I'm just not used to having someone in my life that cares."

Noah's eyes held a glint as he sent Sam an impish grin. "Maybe you should get used to it, Samantha Blacker. I *do* care about you."

Warmth flowed over Sam and filled her with happiness, but she still had something else on her mind. She always suspected that people who went to church never had to face troubles and were somehow protected from bad things happening to them that wasn't their doing. She blurted out, "Why does God allow stuff like this happen to people?"

Noah instantly straightened, aware Sam was confused and needed an answer. "Sam, I don't believe God lets bad things happen. We live in a world where everyone has problems. Some situations are accidental and others we bring on because of bad choices.

"You've heard Pastor Stevens. The devil has this world wrapped around his finger. Even so, I do know God is there for us to help us get through the problems we face in life.

"The Bible tells us in Matthew Five that we are his children, all of us. Sam, we all have to deal with bad things no matter who we are or even if we walk daily with God."

Watching a sad expression cloud her face, he went on, "You can't lose hope, because the Bible tells us in Romans Eight that all things will work together if we love God. Just read your Bible and let him work in your heart. God takes care of us, but we have to believe in Him."

Sam listened, taking in what Noah said. "Even with what has happened, Noah, I still want to learn more about God. There's a lot I have trouble understanding."

Sam gulped in a breath, telling herself she needed to think about what he said.

"I guess this would be one of those times when Bo would say just turn things over to Jesus and believe in him."

"Exactly." Noah turned to go. He pitched an amused grin Sam's way and wiggled his eyebrow. "Sam, when you get out of here, I need a few weeks to make up. I've missed holding you in my arms."

Back in her cell, Sam propped herself against the cold cement wall, praying while she meditated on the things that Noah had said.

Noah couldn't wait to get back home, call his uncle and ask him what he could do to help Sam.

Noah listened to the awkward silence as his uncle hesitated before responding. "I'll have to check into matters. I'm scheduled to talk with the judge on Monday. Perhaps he'll agree to grant her bail."

Noah's heart swelled with hope. "I want to be there, Uncle Frank. Sam is a very special woman to me."

Frank Cane paused again, then replied, "I sort of figured she was. You normally don't ask me to help someone on a case in Big Fork Lake."

"Uncle Frank, what does Sheriff Gruver say?"

"Noah, you know I really shouldn't say a lot about the case, but I don't suppose Sam would mind. The report filed states that he was poisoned by the alkaloid taxane, found in the seeds of yew berries. The evidence they have points to Sam. Her fingerprints are the only ones in the room other than his."

Noah concentrated on picturing the berries. "Those are grape-size berries that come from yew bushes—the ones that resemble a Christmas tree."

Noah's uncle agreed. "They found a half-eaten slice lying on the bathroom floor."

Noah wished he could just fix Sam's problems for her. "I wonder where the berries came from."

"Noah, I don't know. Sam says she doesn't know anything about the berries and that she ordered blueberry pies from a supplier in Montgomery."

Relief flooded Noah. "Okay, there's the answer."

"No Noah, I'm afraid not. They searched the inn and her apartment. They didn't find any invoice showing an order nor did they find blueberry pies."

Later that evening, Belle came to see Sam. "Belle, you didn't have to come here."

Ignoring Sam's response, she blurted out, "I just had to see if you were okay. Are you?"

Sam let out a little laugh at the irony of that. She knew everyone meant well, but she was getting tired of people making that remark. "I'm as good as can be. Mr. Cane is going to get a bail hearing set up. Belle, thanks for calling Noah."

Belle glanced around the cold ugly room then back at Sam. "I didn't know who else to call. I know he cares for you. I can see it on his face."

As bad as Sam felt, Belle's comment lifted her spirits once more. "Is everything okay at the inn?"

Hesitating, she answered, "We have guests checking out early. I think all this is making them edgy."

Sam solemnly focused on those words. She'd figured her customers would react to the murder. "How's Anne doing?"

Belle tightened her ponytail while she answered. "Oh, you know Anne. She's tough. Sam, you just worry about getting out of here. Now tell me how things are with you and Noah."

Sam's face crinkled with a wide smile. "One good thing has come out of this. We're back together."

A look of satisfaction crossed the young woman's face. "Sam, that's great."

Sam barely heard the remark as she talked on, filling her friend in on Noah. "I told him about seeing the older model truck lurking around. He said I should have told him earlier. I'm just not used to having someone who wants to share things."

Belle left and Sam's spirits lifted. She did feel a little more optimistic.

She lay on the hard bunk. With all her might, she prayed she only had one more night in this smelly, grubby room. Maybe then she could go home.

On Monday, Sam received a message from Mr. Cane that the hearing wouldn't be until Tuesday. He spoke with uncertainty as what the judge might do, but Sam held on to hope as the hours slipped away bit by bit.

CHAPTER SEVEN

Tuesday morning, Sam was determined to stay positive. Sitting beside Mr. Cane, she twisted her hands together as she glanced around the room.

The judge addressed Sam and inquired as to what her plans were.

Sam stood straight and focused on being brave, even if her insides were swirling around like a whirlpool. "Sir, I am staying in Big Fork Lake and running the inn."

The judge peered over his notes at Sam with improbability. "I understand that the will for your estate says you only have to stay a year."

Directly, without even the slightest hesitation, Sam replied, "Yes, that's what the will says, but I've decided to stay and make Big Fork Lake my home. I enjoy the inn and can't see myself anywhere else now."

As the judge scanned his document, he stated in a flat voice, "You have no relatives or any reason for me to believe you, Ms. Blacker."

Noah shifted in his seat where he sat behind his uncle. Quietly, he leaned and tapped Frank on the shoulder. "Uncle Frank, I want to speak to the judge."

Without responding, Frank stood. "May we speak your honor?"

"Yes, Mr. Cane, you may."

"Thank you, sir. Mr. Noah Frye wishes to address the court."

The judge turned his attention to Noah. "Very well, continue."

Sam listened in anticipation, praying Noah would say something that would help her.

Noah planted his feet, holding his hands behind his back as he addressed the judge. "Sir, I've lived in Big Fork Lake all my life. I presently work with the county as inspector. I would like to request that the court consider letting Ms. Blacker out on bail. I will vouch for her as a stable person in Big Fork Lake. I've known her the entire time she has lived here."

The judge leaned back in his chair, his eyes reviewing Sam. Then he turned his attention to Noah. "Mr. Frye, what if I let her out and she skips bail?"

Noah lifted his head and shifted in a positive stance. "Sir, I don't believe Ms. Blacker will do that."

The judge focused on Sam with uncertainty. "Murder is a substantial charge, Mr. Frye."

"Yes sir, but I believe she is innocent and I am sure that Sam wants a chance to prove that to all the people in the community."

The stern looking man took a moment, glancing at all three of them, and then inquired, "Ms. Blacker, is there anything else you wish to add?"

Sam stood stiff. Silently she steadied her nerves, knowing she needed to make a convincing statement. "I am innocent, your Honor, and I'm not going anywhere. No matter what happens with this trial, I plan on staying in Big Fork Lake."

The judge studied all three of them once more, then announced, "We will meet at two o'clock at which time I will have a verdict."

Before two, Anne stopped by to visit. Sam noticed the change in her expression—there was no denying the kindness Anne expressed as she inquired about matters.

"Anne, I didn't do anything."

Anne made a gesture of belief toward Sam. "Sometimes things happen we just don't understand."

Sam's mind shifted to her business. "Anne, how is everything at the inn?"

Looking down at the floor, Anne sniffed in the air. "Right now, things are slow. A few of the guests have left early. I just don't know what the next few months will hold for us. I've told everyone that it is not our fault and I will make sure the food is good even if I have to taste every bite myself."

Sam's face widened with humor, knowing that was just like something Anne would say. "Thanks, Anne. I know that helps—you are a fixture in Big Fork Lake and people trust you."

Two o'clock arrived and Sam faced the judge. She gave a side-glance toward Frank Cane and silently prayed to God to help her.

A catch in her breath caused her to momentarily close her eyes as she awaited her fate, at least for now anyway.

"Ms. Blacker, after reviewing your file, I found nothing of any significance. You have no previous record except for a parking ticket. Given that and the fact that Mr. Frye vouched for you, I will grant you bail. However, it will be on one condition.

"Mr. Cane, your client must call into our office every day."

Frank addressed the judge with a nod. "I'm sure Ms. Blacker will follow the regulations as instructed, sir."

The judge banged his gavel and announced firmly, "The bail is set at seventy-five thousand dollars. When that is paid, she is free to go. Mr. Cane we will contact you on the continuing events. Court is dismissed."

Noah looked to her in concern. "Are you okay, Sam? This is good news."

Sam was at a total loss. Could things get any worse? What was she going to do? "Yes, I am, but I guess I'm stuck in jail until the trial date."

Frank came to a sudden halt and gazed at Sam. "Why would that be?"

Her sadness deepened while she searched for a way to explain. Finally, Sam decided to be honest with them both. "Mr. Cane, I don't have seventy-five thousand dollars. I'll never have a way to get that kind of money."

Noah eased closer to Sam. "You don't have to pay all the seventy-five thousand dollars. Just a percent, to show that you intend to stay around."

Sam's day was beginning to wear on her as she threw an aggravated gawk toward him. "Noah, I've less than forty-five hundred in my account. I will not take out of the inn's account."

Noah pitched an intense look at his Uncle.

Apparently, Frank understood what Noah's expression conveyed. He nodded a show of approval.

"Sam, I will not let you stay in jail."

Then Frank interjected, "Sometimes these things take a while to go to court. Could drag out eight or nine months."

Sam's throat closed with a lump. She swallowed hard, fighting the yearning to flee. "Eight months before this is going to end!"

"Yes Sam, I am afraid so, but that will give us time to prepare a good defense."

She shook her head, unsure of what to do when she heard Noah lightly tapping his foot on the floor.

She shot them both a defiant stare. "No Noah, you can't do that."

Lowering his voice, Noah announced firmly, "Sam, don't be stubborn. Let me help you. I will not have you staying in jail for eight months. If you want, you can call this a loan." With a sigh, he lightened the tone of his voice and grinned. "I know a lawyer who will draw up an agreement."

Sam's eyes shifted back and forth at them both, not sure what to do. She wanted to get out of jail, but after all that'd happened, she didn't want Noah suspecting she was the kind of woman who used a man for his money.

Frank noted her qualms as he spoke. "Sam, you can pay him back once all this is over."

She hung her head and knew this was the only choice. "Are you sure, Noah?"

Noah shook his head in assurance. "Yes Sam, I want to do this. Come on, let's go and get you out of here."

Later that night, Sam and Noah cuddled on her couch. Relief flooded Sam just to be out of jail. She laid her head on Noah's shoulder and rested in the warmth of his body seeping through his shirt.

"Noah, how is your uncle going to prove I am innocent? This just looks bad."

Noah tightened his embrace and rubbed Sam's shoulder. "He's a good lawyer, Sam, but sometimes cases can take a while to go to court. He'll check into everything and contact you to talk more.

"In the meantime, you have to keep on going every day. Place your faith in God. He will guide us to the truth."

Sam sat silently. Her skin tingled as Noah's fingers drew circles on her arm. She contemplated what Noah said. Her heart wanted to believe he was right. "I will try, Noah, but I'm scared."

"I know, dear. It's okay to be afraid, just keep your faith. You've had a long weekend. Even though I would love to stay and hold you all night, I'm going so you can get some rest."

Noah seductively cupped Sam's butt as they stood at the door saying goodbye.

She held on to him tightly, not wanting him to go. Just as she was about to ask him to stay, she spotted something over his shoulder.

Swallowing, she tightened her arms around him.

Lurking in the shadows was the old truck parked halfway in the shallow side ditch.

Sam turned her face to his neck and whispered, "That truck is sitting across the road."

Hugging Sam one last time, he whispered in her ear and hurriedly walked to his truck.

Noah seated himself in his vehicle, careful not to glance in the direction of the black object. He wanted to make whoever was sitting in the truck believe he was leaving.

After going for a mile, he turned around and doubled back. Approaching the front of the inn, he inspected the area, shaking his head in aggravation at the empty spot. The old truck was nowhere in sight.

He couldn't help but worry about Sam and wonder why this was happening.

Pulling his vehicle closer to the curb, he turned off the engine and settled in, knowing this was going to be a long night.

While the hours slowly ticked away, he couldn't help but question things. If the Lord led Sam to him, then what was His plan for them both?

He gazed into the darkness and watched the parking lot.

Glancing toward Sam's window, Noah remembered the scripture that promises, "All things work out for good for those who love the Lord."

Hours later, Noah rubbed his weary eyes and slowly pulled his truck on to the road to head home. He was more determined than ever to trust God to bring the truth into the light so he could have a future with Sam one day.

CHAPTER EIGHT

The next morning, Sam trotted down the stairs. Anne and Belle peered toward her as she descended the last step.

Belle broke into a smile that beamed across her face. "Sam, I'm so glad you are home."

Just the sight of Belle's face lighting up put a song in Sam's heart. "Hi Belle! Boy is it great to see you both."

Anne grinned as she eyed Sam. "Sam, good to have you back. So they let you off the hook?"

Pausing, Sam wavered. Then she remembered how small Big Fork Lake is. People in little towns were supposed to be more open with each other. "No Anne. Noah put up the bail and I am going to pay him back."

That week, Sam watched painfully as the remaining guests slowly checked out. Not only were they leaving early, but the cancellations had started to roll in.

Over the next few weeks, some of the regular town people still stopped by, but many stayed away from Sam and the inn.

She was glad she'd put most of her money in the inn's account. She would make it through this. Her living upstairs helped. That cut down on her everyday expenses.

She and Noah had returned to their Saturday routine of going out. Noah now spent more time at the inn.

Even though she had a different kind of relationship with Noah, she didn't doubt the attraction that had grown deep and simmered between them.

Sam grinned when Noah popped into her mind. She could sense the way he battled with the passion that pulled at him. Tension oozed when he stepped out of her arms.

She did enjoy being in his arms and was sure it was just a matter of time before she melted his resolve.

In church, she received great comfort in knowing that Pastor Stevens stood by her. The congregation kept her on the prayer list and constantly told her they were asking God to lead them to the truth.

Facing the end of July, Sam and Belle talked about the past summers at the inn.

Belle's voice wavered while she stacked cups. "Well, Sam, usually the inn stays busy until around October. Then in the winter months, we only stayed open three days a week. We host celebrations around the holidays too, just to keep the inn festive."

Trying to lighten the mood, she added, "Hang in there, everything will be okay. Once you're exonerated, everything will get back to normal."

The next day Anne called to tell Sam she was sick.

"Anne, you stay home today. You know there aren't any guests. I planned to close early anyway. Mr. Cane is stopping by to talk to me."

"Thanks Sam, I guess I lifted too much. I do need to rest. I'll see you tomorrow."

At lunchtime, Noah stopped by for a roast beef sandwich. "Hi Sam, how are you doing?"

Sam released Noah's hug and inhaled his calming scent. "Things have slowed down a lot Noah. I don't know how long I can work Anne and Belle."

Noah shook his head in understanding. "Sam, you'll do what's needed for the inn. I know that."

"Your uncle is stopping by this afternoon. He said we need to talk about the case."

Putting down his roast beef sandwich, Noah eyed Sam. "I've always trusted my uncle. If there's a way to prove you're innocent, he'll find it. After you've talked to Uncle Frank, can I pick you up? Maybe we could go to the lake for a picnic? We haven't done that lately."

Shaking her head in anticipation, Sam's mood lightened. "I think I would like that. The lake will probably be a much-needed diversion."

Later that afternoon when Frank stopped in, Sam served him some tea and cookies and excused Belle to go home.

"Are you sure, Sam?"

Sam nodded her head. "Yes, I need to speak to Mr. Cane and we haven't had any customers for hours, so there's no reason for you to hang around."

With an afterthought, Sam added, "Everything has slowed down in the last couple months. I may have to make some temporary changes at the inn."

Belle gazed at Sam, apprehension on her face. "Things have slacked up, but it's given Anne time to teach me a few things about cooking."

"*You're* learning to cook?" The few times she'd heard Belle talk about making food, she had the distinct impression her friend would do anything to avoid doing too much in the kitchen.

Sam settled in her chair across from Mr. Cane at a table.

Her chest beat hard as she rubbed her hair in an attempt to hide her nervousness.

She trusted Mr. Cane, but was afraid he was going to tell her something bad. She lived each day unsure of what her future held.

Frank Cane pulled out her file. "Sam, how have you been doing?"

Sam flashed him a lopsided grin as she wondered if he had any news. "Mr. Cane, before I came to this little town I never cared what people thought. Living here has made me realize that we do need to care about one another."

Seeing the uncertainty in her eyes, Frank acknowledged her remark by shaking his head. "Yes Sam, we do. That's what sets us apart. You'll get through this. We just need to keep our faith."

He did like her and hoped he could get a good defense worked out for her case.

Frank reviewed his notes and started the conversation in a serious tone. "I spoke to the District Attorney. They're going to take this to court the week of Christmas."

Sam's heart stalled as she soaked in what he said. Somehow, even knowing the time for the trial was growing closer, she hadn't expected to hear that.

She supposed she still harbored some hope that by a miracle the date would never be placed on the court's calendar.

Frank asked, "Have you found that missing invoice or figured out where the pies vanished to?"

A sick, twisted sensation moved over Sam, causing her stomach to churn. With her head in her hand, she offered her answer. "No, I've no idea what happened to the invoice. I laid the bill in my office and now I can't find it. I called to see if I could get a copy, but I'm still waiting on a return call."

Eyeing her with concern, he continued, "Have you talked to the other ladies about the pies?"

Pressing her lips together, Sam shook her head. "Yes, Belle and Anne both say they don't know anything about the pies. I understand Belle not knowing. She had a dentist appointment that day and it was later in the afternoon before she clocked in. Besides, she hardly ever goes into the freezer for anything.

"Anne assures me she doesn't know anything about them. I just can't understand why she didn't see them."

Sam laid her hand hard on the table out of frustration. "Mr. Cane, I know I'm not crazy. The pies were delivered here and I put them in the freezer."

Frank Cane was at a loss. He needed something more to ensure Sam's defense.

He plied her for anything that might be important. "Was there anyone in the inn that day when you accepted the delivery?"

Sam's mind traveled back. "Oh, yes! There were two of the guests. They were in the corner booth. But I'm not sure they realized anyone came in. The delivery truck pulls around back. I had ordered a dozen pies and I placed two of them on the counter for everyone and put the rest in the freezer." Sam paused before she continued. "Then I went into the office and placed the invoice in my bill box.

"Just a few minutes later, Anne came to my office door and said the technician had come to service the air conditioning units. Unfortunately, he asked me to go with him to the rooms. That occupied the biggest part of the day.

"When I arrived home from the bank that evening, Anne offered to get me a glass of tea." Taking a deep breath, Sam went on. "Mr. Brookshire entered and I checked him in. Then I went up to my apartment to rest."

Writing notes, the well-dressed lawyer glanced at Sam. "So what about the day you found him?"

Sam folded her hands across her lap and attempted to press out the queasiness that stirred in the pit of her stomach. Inside, she struggled with the memory of finding that man crumpled on the floor. No matter how hard she tried, she couldn't get the image from her head.

"Everything went pretty much as usual that morning. After lunch, I started cleaning the cabins. I believe it was around two when I took a break. Belle and I talked for a few minutes, then I went back to finish tiding the rooms."

Giving herself a second, she took in a long wind, determined to get through this. "That's when I walked into room number seven and stumbled over Mr. Brookshire. At first, I panicked and screamed, and then realized I had to call the police."

He closed his notebook and glanced at Sam. "Is there anyone you know of that would want to frame you for murder?"

Taken aback, Sam gave her lawyer a thoughtful stare as she mulled over his question.

"I don't know, Mr. Cane. I don't think so, but I've been seeing an older model truck hanging around a lot."

With a serious concern written on his face, the tall man asked, "What do you mean 'around', Sam?"

She explained some of the details about how she'd seen the older model truck lurking nearby.

Mr. Cane opened his file folder and started to write. "Do you know anyone who drives a truck like that?"

Like a bolt of lightning, a flashback hit Sam. She remembered seeing Rob leave in his truck the night before she left Atlanta—the same kind of vehicle that parked across the road.

"Yes! I'd forgotten until right now. Still, it's too crazy to mention."

Frank clicked his pen. "With what you are facing, everything has to be checked out. No matter how insignificant a detail may seem to you."

"Okay." Sitting straighter in her chair, Sam started to explain. "Mr. Cane, when I lived in Atlanta, my neighbor drove a similar truck. I dated him a few times and then told him I didn't want to see him again. He got upset and I had a few scenes with him. He tried to push his affections on me. I fled my apartment one horrible time when he almost forced his way. I had to take out a restraining order."

Frank's face wrinkled with a curious expression. "Do you suppose he followed you?"

She sucked in air as the thought of Rob brought that old fear back. Apprehensions long since stuffed away now wiggled up to the surface.

After a pause, Sam said, "Gosh, Mr. Cane, I hadn't even thought about that."

"Sam, I want you to tell me all you can about this neighbor you had. I need to find out where he was that Thursday night."

After Sam had given him all the information she could remember, Mr. Cane assured her he would do his best to locate Rob.

CHAPTER NINE

Sam was drained and heartbroken after Mr. Cane left. She hated to think that Rob had found her. What if he was doing all this? What would happen then?

Scrubbing in the shower, Sam furiously pressed her washcloth hard to her skin. She washed until the water ran cold.

Noah showed up a little before six that evening. As he hugged her, he asked God to make everything okay.

He held her close, feeling the tension in her body.

Sam gazed into his eyes, suddenly aware she wanted to see his brown peepers every day for the rest of her life. Would she have that chance or would she end up in jail for a crime she didn't commit?

As she basked in the comfort of Noah's arms, she knew deep in her heart that this man was the one she could spend the rest of her life with. Sam only hoped he would think the same about her one day too.

On the drive to the lake, Sam filled Noah in on the details of her talk with his uncle.

She shared with him about the few incidents she'd faced with Rob when she lived in Atlanta.

They made their way to the far corner of the lake and Noah tossed a blanket on the ground. Sam settled down and searched out the tranquility her visit with Mr. Cane had robbed her of.

She lifted her head and the warm breeze blew across her face. The late sun beamed hot on the back of her neck.

Finally, she managed to relax a bit. "This is such a nice evening. I don't believe I could pick a better one."

Noah watched the boats in the distance and replied, "No, I couldn't either. This is God's beauty at work. Did Uncle Frank say he would find that guy from Atlanta?"

Though she didn't want to be pulled back to the conversation, she reluctantly answered. "He said he wanted to check him out and determine where he was that night."

Looking carefully at Sam, Noah said, "Do you suspect he followed you here?"

The blood drained from Sam's face as she thought about Rob being in Big Fork. "I hope not, but he might have."

Noah slid closer to her. "Sam, if you see that truck again, you give me a call. Even at two in the morning. I don't want him hurting you anymore. As long as I'm around, he won't get to you."

Hearing the tenderness laced with protectiveness in his voice, she beamed a smile and immersed herself in the embrace of having someone in her life who cared so much. "I will, Noah. I'm just concerned about the trial. Christmas is only four months away."

Taking Sam's chin in his hand, he lightly kissed her. "I know you are. Remember what I said, Sam, believe and have faith."

The rest of the evening they spent eating the picnic Noah had packed and enjoying the beauty of the outdoors.

Every so often, Noah would kiss Sam and leave her to wonder where he really wanted to fit into her life. For a while, Sam just sat quietly and soaked in the calm evening, trying to enjoy the peaceful surroundings.

"Sam, what have you got on your mind?"

"Hum... I was just thinking about things. I get scared sometimes because I don't know where my life is headed."

"I know, Sam. You're in a bad situation right now, but remember that God is always there with you. Somehow, He will lead us through this.

"It's important to have faith. You know God's word says that faith is the substance of things hoped for."

Sam stretched out her legs. "I know, Noah. I have no choice. I want to believe that. There is a verse I like in Psalm 37. It's given my some peace about my situation."

Noah sat and played with a blade of grass, silently giving thanks that Sam was drawing closer to God. "I know many times when I doubt something, Sam, I just go to my Bible. I've learned God's word can be a source of strength. It sure has guided me through the years."

Night moved in and Noah took her home and promised to see her Saturday. They also discussed plans for him to pick her up on Sunday morning for church and lunch after.

From the corner of her eye, Sam thought she might have seen the older vehicle cruise by while she watched Noah leave, but it was probably just her fears causing her to be jumpy. Not being certain, she dismissed the notion.

Saturday morning, Sam placed out a few pastries for the locals and served coffee. She carried on her work. At least she still took pride in the inn and it lifted her spirits to hear words of kindness from some of her new friends that continued to stop by.

Around eleven, she went to clean the rooms a final time. She had made the decision to close the cabins even though there was still a lot of the fishing season left. The way folks had checked out early was proof enough that until this trial was over, no one wanted to stay at the inn.

A few hours into her cleaning, she strolled back to the diner.

Sam used the excuse that she was thirsty, knowing full-well she was just putting off going into that little cabin where she had found Mr. Brookshire's body.

It was hot outside but cold chills still crawled across her back. She poured herself a drink and sipped the amber-colored liquid when the ringing of the telephone broke the silence.

"Noah, I'm glad you called."

Noah pictured Sam's smile as he slowly spoke. "So, how is my favorite lady today?"

She was relieved that Noah called. It gave her another excuse to stay away from that room. "Okay so far, I've been cleaning rooms and storing things. I'm pretty sure I won't have any more guests until this murder trial is over."

The tenderness in Noah's voice soothed her. "Sam, I know things seem bad. Do you want me to come over and go in room seven with you?"

Her heart leapt as anticipation moved in. She did want his help, very much, but hesitated to require it of him. "I really didn't want to ask you to do that, but I would feel better if someone went with me. I could probably just call Belle and see if she could come over."

Noah quickly responded that he wanted to be the one to accompany Sam. "I'll come over. We'll go in there together, Sam. I have a mess to clean up first before I can come over. I'm repairing a leak in my drain."

Sam paused, remembering Noah mentioning that he rented his house. "The property owner doesn't do that?"

The clank of a wrench sounded. "Sure he does, but when something happens that I can easily take care of, I just repair it myself. Sometimes that's a lot easier than taking time off for a plumber to stop by and half the time, they don't know what they're doing. Anyway, I'm almost finished. I'll be over soon."

Men. Sam frowned and shook her head—she would never understand some of their ways. "I can clean the other rooms while you're doing that. I really appreciate this, Noah."

After they hung up the phone, Noah laughed at himself. No, he didn't need to repair anything, or even rent, for that matter.

The investments he'd made over the years were solid and provided a nice addition to his hefty savings account. At any rate, he figured when he did have a family one day, then they would use the money together.

Two hours later, Noah pulled in the parking lot just as Sam finished the last room.

He stepped out of the truck and walked over to Sam, taking her into his arms. "Are you sure you're up to this?"

Sam's pulse sped in response to his embrace. "Maybe not, but I need to make sure the room is cleaned. I'm hoping for better things next year, so I want everything ready."

While they walked toward the room with the big red number painted on the door, Sam exchanged small talk with Noah, trying to ease her churning nerves.

"I worked on some ads to place in fishing magazines and papers for the inn."

"That's great, Sam. I tried to get Bo to do that. He was old fashioned—he would just say people would come, always have."

Fondness swept over Sam as she recalled something Bo said to her once. Thinking aloud she shared, "He would talk about trusting. Every year when I saw him, he shared his belief about the mercy Jesus has for us. I wonder what Bo would say to me now if he could see what was going on."

Noah stopped and turned his attention on Sam. "Bo would tell you not to give up and trust in God."

Standing in front of the threshold Sam knew she had to cross, she nodded. "Yes, I know you're right."

Going into the room, she focused hard to keep her composure. Despite all her efforts, her eyes navigated to the spot on the floor where she had found Mr. Brookshire.

Sam's heart did a triple catch and sent a knot to her throat. She forced control and turned her head quickly.

Despite all, her knees grew feeble and started to buckle. The room spun like a top.

Noah noticed Sam as she began to sway and hurriedly circled her with his arms to keep her from falling.

Gently, he laid her head on his shoulder. "Everything will be all right."

Slightly weaving in his arms, Sam rested her head, gathering strength from his embrace. "Yes, I'll be okay. It's just hard to accept that all this has happened."

Noah clutched her more securely, wishing he knew some way to give her his inner strength. His heart reached out to her—he wanted to fix it all, but didn't know how.

After a few minutes, Noah kissed Sam's head, bringing her focus on him as he gazed into her eyes.

Smiling, Noah remembered the first day he saw Sam and those big blue eyes of hers.

"Sam, does the carpet need shampooed?"

Forcing a resolve she didn't really believe she had, Sam skimmed the room, concentrating her focus on anything but that one spot of the floor. "Yes, that's the most important thing we need to do."

Noah walked outside the door and pushed the carpet cleaner inside. "While I clean the carpet, you strip the bed and clean the counter and coffee pot."

Sam wobbled her head in wonder and gave a doubtful smile. "Do you even know how to use that thing?"

His eyes got big as he pretended to be upset. "Do you doubt my cleaning capabilities, madam? I use to do this for my mom when I was a young boy."

During the time they worked in the room, she fixed her mind to stay encouraged. The job did grow easier as she concentrated on her work.

Silently she rinsed out the coffee pot and thanked God for Noah's help.

When they finished cleaning the room, she pushed the dirty linen cart in the storage area. "Thanks for the help, Noah. I really don't think I would've been capable of cleaning that little room by myself."

Hand in hand, they walked back toward the inn.

Noah massaged her hand and felt the softness of her skin. "Sam, let me take you out to eat. I say we deserve it."

Sam paused. Her heart hung heavy with a weight she couldn't put into words. "Noah, I just don't think I want to go out tonight."

Noah planned to stand firm. He didn't want to leave her alone, not yet anyway. "Sam, I've made some pretty good meals in my time. How about I stay and fix us something to eat?"

Her senses pricked at the thought. "I didn't know you cooked."

Was he perfect in every way?

Noah gave her a sideways glance and slightly grinned. "I am a single man, so of course I cook. Going out to eat gets old after a while, so I had to learn."

As they stepped inside the inn, Noah released her hand and planted a kiss on her knuckles. "I'll go to the kitchen and get started on something to eat. You go upstairs and freshen up."

While Sam changed her clothes, she contemplated her situation. Finally, she decided that somehow things would work out. No matter what, she would pick up the pieces again, as she had before. She just needed to get out of this mess.

Noah departed behind the counter and entered into the small, long kitchen. Opening the refrigerator, he found some potato salad, sub bread and enough luncheon meats for a sub sandwich.

As he walked to the pantry to get the mustard, his foot crunched something. Stepping back, he bent down to the floor and scooped up a dry, brittle stem of needlelike foliage.

Holding what was left of the greenery, he wondered where the crumbled piece of conifer came from. He couldn't remember seeing any trees with such growth on them before.

Sam walked into the kitchen and interrupted his thoughts.

"Noah, subs. What a good idea."

Noah stopped and gazed at Sam. He recognized her change of voice and was pleased. "Have you got any mustard?"

She grinned and went to the cupboard for the yellow container.

Noah held the dried wrinkled foliage up. "Sam, do you know where this old stem came from?"

She barely glanced at what he was holding. "I don't know? I guess one of us drug it in on our shoes. Funny though, I haven't seen any trees around here that look like that." She shrugged her shoulders. "Who knows?"

Noah picked up the mustard as he seated himself across from Sam. "You relax and let me serve the subs."

Content, Sam watched Noah. She couldn't stop herself from thinking how cute he looked fixing sandwiches.

"You know, Noah, this is nice. Watching you work in the kitchen makes me feel better."

He shot Sam a mischievous grin and placed a sub in front of her. "All you need is one of my famous sub sandwiches." Prideful, he continued, "I make the best in Big Fork Lake."

She reached down and took a bite and mocked the expression of shock then grinned at him. "I do have to say, they are good, and so is the company."

After the sandwiches, Sam pushed up and started to clear the table.

Noah slipped out of his chair, turning Sam's attention from the mess. Naughtiness showed on his face as he tackled Sam to the counter.

She felt Noah's hands caress her curves. Her mind strayed away from all thoughts of food.

Sam bathed in the warmth of his muscular body that held her tight. She wrapped her fingers in his hair, tangling the stubborn tendrils. Her thoughts drifted. Boy, he had a way of melting away any tension that lingered.

That night on the way home, Noah couldn't seem to get the old crumpled leaf out of his mind. What was this obsession with the dirty old thing? Why he would let something like dead foliage bother him?

Where had he noticed those trees before?

A memory nudged at him that he couldn't retrieve.

Finally, he put any thoughts of the greenery to rest. As Sam said, it was just something someone drug in.

Monday, Sam greeted the usual small amount of locals that came in for coffee and some of Anne's muffins.

From the kitchen, Belle hollered to Sam, "There's a call for you!" Sam politely finished her conversation with one of her neighbors and walked into her office.

Answering the phone, Sam listened in shock as an older woman on the line filled her in on the news.

"You can't find the invoice for the pies I ordered?"

The gravelly voice slowly responded, "No, Ms. Blacker. The driver was new and he didn't make carbon copies of the deliveries for that week."

Every nerve tensed as Sam responded. She'd hung her hopes on this one thing. Without the pies, this was the only other proof she had to back up her story. "Isn't there any other way you can verify that the man made a delivery at the inn?"

The lady on the other end of the line retorted apologies. "I am afraid not, other than if the driver remembered stopping at the inn."

Breathing a sigh of relief, Sam continued, "Okay, so he can do that."

After a pause, a scratchy reply rang in her ears. "I am sorry, Ms. Blacker. That's impossible."

Sam was so close to getting what she needed, she began to lose her patience. "Maybe if I talk to him, he will remember stopping by here."

"Ms. Blacker, he only worked that week and didn't show back up. When we tried to call him, we couldn't get a working number. I'm sorry, but we don't have any way of getting in touch with him."

Sam hung up the phone and walked to the window, staring out at nothing. Her mind focused on the invoice and pies from Top's Warehouse.

Mentally, she created a list of people who would have known she put the pies in the freezer. Anne, at the very least.

Why would anyone take them out?

Belle poked her head in the office door. "Sam, Anne wanted to know if you need her to make sandwiches for lunch?"

Speaking to Belle, Sam kept her back toward her. "Yes, but just a dozen. After that, the three of us need to have a much needed talk."

A short while later, Sam strode into the dining room of the inn as Anne served the three of them roast beef sandwiches. "Are you okay, Sam?"

Putting on a facade, she slapped a smile across her face and motioned for Anne to sit down. "Yes, I'm just upset. I thought I would be able to get a copy of the delivery invoice for those pies, but I won't be able to do that."

Eyeing Sam with worry, Anne sighed, "Oh Sam, I'm sorry."

Something in the tone of Anne's voice and the way she reacted, almost as if in relief, made Sam blurt out, "Anne, are you *sure* you didn't see the pies? I put them in the freezer."

Anne questioned her with her facial expression as she wiggled her head back and forth. "No, I don't know anything about those pies, Sam. Why in the world would should I?"

Sam lowered her voice just above a whisper and replied, "Because Anne, it's only you, Belle, and I here. I signed for them and put them in the freezer."

Anne narrowed her eyes. "Sam, I hope you're right. There was a lot going on that day."

Sam bit her tongue and cocked her head sternly in the heat of agitation. Only reminding herself that Anne was older stopped her from lashing out. Even though she did like Anne, she had to admit Anne was an odd sort.

Through gritted teeth, Sam's voice came out laden with irritation. "Yes, Anne, I am sure."

Anne's face sported a downhearted look as she laid her hand on Sam's shoulder. "Sam, I'm sorry for all the misery you're going through."

Before Anne could leave the table, Sam motioned for Belle to join them.

As Belle seated herself across from Anne, Sam glanced back and forth at them both. "I really hate to make this decision, but we need to cut hours until things get better."

Anne slumped in her seat, dread on her face. "Sam, are we fired?"

Shocked by her remark, Sam turned toward Anne. "No, I want you both to work here, but a lot of people have stopped coming and we just don't have enough business to keep busy. The trial will be coming in December. I hope this can be cleared up by the end of January."

Anne turned her head toward the wall. "That sounds all well and good Sam, but what if things don't work out the way you want them to? What will you do with the inn then?"

Emotionally, Sam's insides turned. Anne's remark threatened to crush any dreams she had. "Anne, I'm not doing anything with the inn. This is my home. I've enjoyed running the inn, but it doesn't matter if I get to open for business or not, I'm staying here. If I needed to, I could ask Noah to keep an eye on the place for me."

Anne studied Sam with a saddened expression. "I'm not ready to retire, but I guess I can use the free time to spruce my house up."

Belle frowned with uncertainty and finally spoke up. "I might be able to get a hired on temporarily with my cousin at the theater."

"Thanks." Sam hesitated a second before adding. "This place just wouldn't be the same without the two of you."

Sam placed the closed sign up and under the big red letters she used a marker to add *Until the end of January*. She felt down after the conversation with the ladies, but wasn't ready to give up. Not just yet anyway. Back in her office, she thought about the invoice from Top's warehouse. Determined to find it, she started searching.

She rummaged through every drawer and shelf and moved about in her office pushing furniture as she rearranged.

Spent with exhaustion, she slumped in her chair. Her thoughts pursued areas she may have missed.

She knew the paperwork had to be there somewhere.

She didn't understand how pies could go missing either, but they had, and she needed to find some proof.

Sunday came and Noah picked Sam up for church. Sam rested in the pew beside Noah, listening to Pastor Stevens as he preached about Jesus and Peter.

She found herself drawn to the sermon of how Peter fell in the water when he took his eyes off Jesus and put his mind on the troubles that surrounded him.

Pastor Stevens continued to preach and overwhelming need surfaced.

She realized she had spent too much time with her eyes on her troubles and not enough time trusting in the Lord. Sam's heart opened, pouring out a longing to get closer to Jesus and his mercy.

She wanted to become a child of God.

At the end of his sermon, Pastor Stevens made the alter call.

Sam stood and bit by bit, her shaky legs moved. Finally, she was positioned at the front of the church. She didn't understand, but somehow she knew that now was the time to accept Jesus in her life.

Somewhere in her soul, she believed that God did forgive her, and he was calling to her even with all her imperfections.

Pastor Stevens eyed Sam as she approached. Silently, he thanked God for bringing her into his fold. "Yes Sam, what is your need?"

Shyly, Sam clasped her hands together. A timid mood clouded her. "Pastor, I would like to ask God to forgive me. I believe it's time I dedicated my life to him."

Sam repeated the prayer of forgiveness and asked the Lord to come into her heart.

She wanted a new life with a clean slate.

Sensations rushed through her as she made her way back to her seat. Sam couldn't explain the compassion. Her heart hammered with excitement and at the same time, a gentle peace flowed through her body.

Silent tears trickled down her cheeks.

Then an instant later, she felt a joy she couldn't explain. Sam's face beamed as she thought about God and who she was now. A Christian.

A new sense of contentment washed over her. She felt as if a weight lifted right off her shoulders.

Sam knew everything was the same, but somehow, things were different. A transformation she couldn't put into words, but was there, in her innermost being. For the first time in her life, Sam understood that God would take care of her.

After the church service was over, everyone came to Sam and offered support.

Noah stood alongside of her and quietly gushed with pride. He opened the truck door, joy shining in his heart. "I believe we need to celebrate."

He scooted in his seat and grinned. He wiggled his eyebrows and added in a playful manner, "Watch out lady, you might be called a Christian now."

Sam busted into laughter as they pulled out and headed down the road.

They enjoyed a light lunch then went to Noah's house. All during the day, Sam bathed in the idea of always being with Noah.

Still, she couldn't help the nagging words that played in the back of her mind. She had to wonder if anything more permanent would ever happen between them.

She believed Noah cared for her, but she couldn't begin to guess what he really wanted out of life. Would he ever wish to totally devote himself to her?

In the afternoon, they enjoyed a dinner together before heading back to church.

Noah stared at Sam. She didn't realize that God had also answered his prayer.

He had put his faith in God that if Sam was the woman for him, then she would eventually come to know Jesus as her savior.

That night when Noah took Sam home, they talked about the day that would live in her mind forever. Before he left, he enfolded her in his arms. "You know, it's getting harder to leave you."

"Is it Noah? I like that."

Noah put his hand on the back of her neck as he tenderly spoke. "I like that you like that. I want us to move forward together. When the time is right, I know we will."

CHAPTER TEN

Noah backed out of her driveway and turned his head toward the trees. There, across the road, he saw a dark shape parked in the dimness, concealed only by the tree limbs that hung low.

As he turned around in the empty parking lot of Big Fork Inn & Eats, he decided to end this for good. Whoever was in the truck had some explaining to do. His headlights shined across the road to the spot where the vehicle hid. In a flash, the old truck skidded out. Noah sped from the lot and followed.

Despite determination, somehow he lost the vehicle. He circled back and drove down a few of the many side roads that led to boat docks and clearings made for fishing. The night was dark, without any stars in the sky, and the truck could have hid anywhere. Finally, he faced the fact that the old pickup had disappeared.

Noah tossed in bed. Finally, he gave up trying to sleep and turned on his lamp. He knew couldn't rest until he called and made sure Sam was all right.

"Hi Sam, are you okay?"

Half-asleep, Sam muttered, "Yes Noah, I'm fine. What's wrong?"

Noah quickly decided not to upset her. "I just wanted to make sure everything's okay and say goodnight."

The following Wednesday, Mr. Cane called Sam. "Sam, I have some bad news. The police can't locate Rob. The property owner stated he left owing three months worth of rent. Apparently, he just packed up and took off one day. Evidently, he was kin to her because she mentioned that her sister wasn't even sure where he was."

Sam clutched her chest. A sick feeling covered her—no one knew where he was. That wasn't good. "So that's it then. We don't know anything."

"I am afraid not, but don't be discouraged. He may or may not be the one following you. We don't know for sure. Sam, the next time you see that vehicle try to get a tag number then call the sheriff and report it. I'm working on some other things, so keep up your faith."

Sam mechanically replied, "Okay Mr. Cane, I'll try."

"How is the search for the invoice coming?"

Sam jerked back to the moment and wished she had better news. "Not good. I can't find that paper anywhere. I've even checked my apartment, although I know I didn't take it home with me. I can't get a copy of it either. The receptionist said that the delivery man for this area quit. They didn't have any forwarding information on him."

"Sam, you need to keep trying. That invoice would tighten your case. Call me if you think of anything else."

Before hanging up the phone, all she managed to say was, "I will. Thank you."

The next Friday, Noah stopped by the inn and stared in amazement at Sam. She had trash bags flung around and debris scattered everywhere.

"Hi Noah, I'm glad you stopped by. I was a little down in the dumps and decided I would keep myself busy by doing some cleaning."

He peered in the room with bewilderment.

The inside of the inn resembled an area where someone was preparing to move.

With uncertainty in his voice, he said, "I got off early today, so I wanted to come by and see you. What in the world are you doing, Sam?"

Following Noah's eyes to the trash and boxes she'd scattered around, she smiled.

"I'm only cleaning up the pantry, kitchen and storage closet. Those rooms needed a thorough cleaning. I decided I would make sure everything was tidy for the coming winter."

Noah scratched his head. Still thinking she needed a break, he remarked, "It isn't winter yet, Sam."

Taking Noah by the arms, she ignored his obvious concern and led him to the pantry. "Can you help me slide the freezer away from the wall? Who knows the last time this cooler has been swept behind?"

Standing there, Noah watched Sam as she worked. While she pushed her broom back and forth she talked. "I want to get this place looking better. Since I've been here I haven't had the chance to clean everything out."

Noah walked over and gazed out the window.

Sam assaulted his thoughts when she shrieked, "Oh my God! Noah."

He snapped to attention and whirled toward Sam. "What is it Sam? Did you see a rat?"

Sam jumped around in circles swinging a square cardboard box. "Noah this is one of the pie boxes from Top's Warehouse."

She grabbed Noah, dancing around, very elated at her find.

Noah embraced her, thanking God for helping her find the empty pie box.

Suddenly, she jerked out of his clasp. "Sam, what's wrong?"

Turning to run to the office, she yelled over her shoulder, "I need to call Mr. Cane!"

The rest of the evening, Sam danced on cloud nine. Now that she knew Noah had seen the pie box, she felt so much better—at least Noah and Mr. Cane knew she wasn't lying.

Noah returned home and called his uncle. "Sam sure was excited about that box. Uncle Frank, will the container help her case?"

"It may help, Noah, especially with the delivery date printed on the side. At least now her story has credibility. This will be a good point for our side. I told her to inform me if anything else comes up, no matter how small. Sometimes all the little things pieced together makes the case."

As Noah paced around his kitchen, he confided in his uncle. "I am just a little concerned, Uncle Frank. I know in my heart she didn't murder anyone. I want this whole mess to be finished.

"Just between you and I, I've waited on a woman like her all my life. Uncle Frank, she's the one I want to spend the rest of my life with, but I haven't told her yet."

Noah's uncle listened then responded in a stern voice. "Noah, if that's the way you feel then don't wait until it is too late.

"No matter what the outcome of this trial, if Sam is the lady meant to be in your life, things will work out, one way or the other." Softening his tone, he continued, "If you love her, Noah, she needs to be told. Life is too short not let someone know how much you care."

Halloween came. Sam and Noah went to the church's fall festival to help with the games and hand out treats dressed in Biblical costumes.

Sam dressed as Martha and Noah choose a costume that represented Peter. Ever since that day the Pastor preached about

Peter in church and Sam had asked the Lord into her life, Noah had established a fondness for Peter.

They had volunteered to help with the apple-bobbing tub. Sam laughed at Noah as he got wet when he helped a little boy get an apple out of the tub.

"Noah, this is fun. I never did anything like this in Atlanta."

He dried the water off his face and smiled. "Big Fork Worship Center has always tried to make Halloween safe and a positive, Christian experience for the kids so they don't feel left out. It's just a part of helping the community. I'd hoped you would enjoy tonight."

Sam filled the tub up with more apples and scanned the room.

"Thanks. The evening has certainly taken my mind off what's coming up in a couple of months."

Noah reached out and claimed Sam's hand. "Sam, you will get past this and I'll be here for you." As her gave her a quick kiss, he said, "I'll be right back. We need more apples."

Sam found herself thinking about how she felt so at home in Big Fork Lake. Even with all the problems she had right now, she was satisfied. How things had changed in less than a year.

Yes, something bad had happened, but something good had also happened. She had found God and Noah and she had a home.

Sam smiled as she saw Belle approach with a little girl dressed in white. "Hi, who is this pretty little angel?"

Belle rubbed the girl's long wheat-colored hair. "This is my niece. I always take her trick-or-treating. We stopped in on the way to Anne's house."

During the conversation, Sam told Belle that she was going to cook a Thanksgiving dinner for Noah. As they chatted, Sam wistfully glanced at the child several times.

Belle told Sam how her temporary job was going. Sam promised Belle she would call her back to work as soon as she could. "I still need you to help me with the inn if I ever get out of this mess I'm in. I couldn't manage without you."

Belle took the small girl's hand as she talked. "Sam, you'll get out of this. Just keep your faith."

Sam stretched her feet out as she rode home in Noah's truck. Satisfaction loomed. For the first time in a while, she believed she'd done something good to help someone. "Noah, I really enjoyed this night."

"Having you with me meant a lot. I'm glad you wanted to share something I feel so strongly about doing. For years, I've helped the church try to make Halloween a little safer for the kids." With a change of subject, he said, "Sam, I'm going to Montgomery tomorrow. Would you go with me?"

A thought crept in Sam's mind. Things were good with her and Noah. Still, she wished she knew how he really felt about her. She couldn't help but wonder if he was ashamed of her because of the trial.

Pushing that aside, she decided to enjoy the time she had with him. "Yes Noah, I'd like that. Why are you going?"

Noah turned on the road that led to the inn. "I thought I'd get another vehicle. I've driven this for years. Time for a change."

He pulled in Sam's drive. In the truck, they held on to each other as Noah's kisses warmed her blood several degrees. His breathing labored as he ran his hands across her body.

Her heart fluttered as she once again wondered what Noah really wanted out of their relationship.

On the way home, Noah second-guessed his decision. He'd almost told Sam he loved her. It was getting harder to leave her. Yes, he wanted Sam and he wanted to be a husband to her one day.

As he contemplated what his uncle had said to him, a Bible verse came to mind about trusting in the Lord with understanding and not always relying on your own way of thinking. He remembered that scripture was in Proverbs. A calming peace circled him as he murmured, "Thank you God. I needed you to remind me."

Just then, he knew what to do. He realized he had to tell Sam that he loved her. He only hoped her knowing would give her more strength to get through this trial.

Sam woke early the next morning. She enjoyed the country mornings—she'd gotten into the habit of rising to the sounds of birds chirping. She especially liked to see the sunrise.

As she relaxed at the table beside the window, she searched out the birds in the distance. She watched them fly over the lake. The trees swayed as a slight breeze blew through their tops.

Life in a small town was certainly different. Who would have believed that such simple things could be so comforting?

Noah arrived early and they traveled the twenty minutes to Montgomery.

After they had breakfast at Waffle Chef, they went to the mall. Sam enjoyed holding hands with Noah as they took their time and checked out the sales in the stores.

She and Noah shopped until the afternoon. Sam glanced in the shop windows. This was the first time she had gotten to see all the storefronts—the last time she was in the mall with Noah was at night and much of the shopping area had been closed.

This mall was smaller than she was used to in the city, but the center still boasted just about any boutique a girl—or guy—could want. Sam was amazed at the variety of stores enclosed in the middle area—a music store, gift shops and even a bridal boutique.

Sam smiled as they left the parking lot. So far, the day had been busy, and now she and Noah were headed to several car dealerships in the area.

Sam had the distinct impression that Noah would be picky about any vehicle he purchased. She was right.

Finally, after three car lots, Noah narrowed the choice down to a couple SUVs.

"Sam, what do you think? Which one should I get?"

She held up her hand to shade her eyes from the sun. "I can't help you make that decision, Noah."

"Yes, you can. That's one reason I asked you to come with me. I wanted you to help me decide."

Noah walked over to Sam to convince her that he needed her input. He angled his head and gazed at the sticker on the window of one of the vehicles.

"If you had shopped all day for a new vehicle, which one would you get?"

She laughed at his remark. "I *have* been on this little expedition with you the whole day."

A haze of uncertainty seemed to cover her face. Then finally, she studied the two vehicles that he had his eyes on. "I like them both. The white one has nice suede interior and fancy wheels, but the red one is a little smaller. I like the leather seats and sunroof."

In a final gesture, she pointed to the sportier SUV and said, "If I was buying a car, I think I would get the red one."

Laughing, Noah joked, "Sam, you sure? It's not yellow."

Sam threw a playful punch, hitting Noah on the arm. "Hey, stop making fun of my old clunker. My yellow Bug has gotten me this far."

Noah tilted his head, a wide smile crossing his face. "Yes and I am very glad it did. See that you stay here with me, young lady."

Sam planted a small kiss on Noah's lips. "Noah, I told you I am not going anywhere. Big Fork Lake is my home now, no matter what happens."

Noah grabbed Sam in a bear hug. "I think we're very lucky to have you, especially me."

The sales representative approached and Noah informed him they had decided to get the red vehicle.

As they went over the papers in the sales representative's office, Noah examined his reason for getting a new SUV. It was all Noah could do not to tell Sam why he wanted another vehicle.

In his opinion, they had to have something different to drive. One day he hoped they would have a family together. Also, he thought Sam needed a more dependable vehicle. He just prayed that when the time came, she would feel the same way he did.

The representative broke into his thoughts as he slid the paper across the desk for Noah to sign. As they stood outside beside the new car, Noah reached for Sam's hand and placed the keys in her palm. "Will you drive the SUV home?"

Shocked at his request, Sam held the keys with uncertainty. She hesitated before she gave him an answer. Something had nagged her all morning and she had to ask. "Why did you want me to help make this decision?"

Noah's appearance took on a serious air he circled his arms around her and gauged just how much he really wanted to reveal in this moment. "Sam, you know one day I hope we can be together permanently. I wouldn't want to make a decision like this without you."

She inhaled a shaky breath, feeling the tight muscles under his shirt that offered a pleasant distraction. "Noah, I...I'm just not sure I know *how* you feel."

His eyes met hers and pierced her soul as he slowly tucked a lock of her hair behind her ear and traced an imaginary line on her lips with his finger.

A shudder passed through Sam. Did she have the right idea or not? Would Noah ever speak up and outright tell her how he really felt?

For several miles down the road, Sam enjoyed driving what she had labeled as Noah's new toy. She searched over the gages and fondled the soft leather seat. The car was equipped with everything—cruise control, seat warmer, MP3 player and especially a sunroof.

She guided the new vehicle down the highway and promised herself that one day she would afford one. For now, her old car took her where she needed to go. Yes, it suited her needs just fine.

Sam passed by a police officer who had someone on a motorcycle pulled over. Her mind snapped to her ongoing turmoil.

The fear of what lie ahead wiggled past her resolve. *I have to clear myself of the mess I'm in before I can plan anything in my life.*

Sam started to brood over her coming trial. Why had this happened? There was a very real possibility she could go to prison for something she didn't do.

Looking up at the sky, she couldn't help but question God. After all, He knew she didn't kill anyone.

A sick taste formed in her mouth as she continued to dwell on the pending trial. She wondered what it would do to her and Noah.

Sam tightened her lips as she considered different scenarios in her mind—all of them made her hurt inside even more.

The big question that plagued her was what would happen to their relationship if she went to jail? Would she lose him forever?

She broke down, the tears falling hard and swiped vigorously at the wet path that trailed down her cheek.

Sam pulled off the exit to Big Fork Lake. She worked desperately to dry her eyes, determined not to ruin Noah's day. Shaking her head, she forced her mind to clear. She really didn't want to let this get to her—she had to keep her faith.

Back at the driveway of her apartment, Sam slid out of the SUV. "Wow, what a great vehicle. I made a good choice. The car rode like a dream."

Suddenly, with a fast change of attitude, she paused and sighed heavy. "Noah, I think I will say goodbye and go up to lie down."

Taken back by the sudden change in her, Noah searched her face with concern. "Are you all right, Sam? Don't you want to ride around the lake with me?"

She slowly wobbled her head, trying to keep her churning stomach at bay. "No, I really did enjoy spending the day with you, but I need to go upstairs and rest. I'll ride in the SUV tomorrow morning when you come to pick me up for church."

He gently touched her head. "Sam, you do look pale. Is there anything I can get you?"

Guilt made her want to be upfront. "Noah, I let myself get stressed today. On the way, back I started to think about the trial and some of the things that could happen."

Noah nodded his head in understanding and embraced her in his arms. "Sam, no bad thoughts. Try to stay strong, honey."

A last thought hit Sam and she looked over the parking lot. "I almost forgot. You can't drive two vehicles home."

Noah glanced over at the new car and smiled. "No, I can't. I'll just take my truck home and in the morning, we will both drive a vehicle to church and afterward swing by my place and leave the truck in my driveway."

Stepping back a little, he gazed into Sam's eyes. "Before I take you to your door, I want to tell you something."

Sam's eyes roamed over his face. The tone in Noah's voice had suddenly changed, causing her to wonder.

Noah circled Sam with his arms, thinking about what he wanted to say. Finally, he backed her up, tenderness lining his face.

He knew at that moment the time had come to tell her how much he loved her. He needed to say the words for both of them to hear. "Sam, I love you."

Sam froze. Did she hear Noah right? "What did you say?"

With more courage, he repeated himself. This time he raised his voice a bit. "I said I love you, Samantha Blacker."

Sam grabbed Noah, planting a kiss on him that spilled out all the love she'd harbored inside for months. Her sick stomach was suddenly all but forgotten—Noah *loved* her.

Giddiness overflowed in Sam. "I was afraid you didn't want me because of the charges against me."

"No, Sam, that's not true. I want you regardless of what might happen. I know the Lord will see us through this."

Sam's smile faltered and her voice crackled. "Noah, what if I get convicted for something I didn't do?"

Noah shook his head no and solemnly remarked, "Then we keep our faith and do what we have to in order to move past it. I promise you, I'm here for you. Sam, I've never felt this way about any woman before."

Noah walked her upstairs and planted a lingering kiss on her lips.

As he turned to go down the steps, he called back over his shoulder. "I love you, Sam."

CHAPTER ELEVEN

Noah called her early just to wish her, "Happy Thanksgiving." Her mood brightened with pleasure as she placed the phone back in the cradle. Sam had never been with anyone who enjoyed the simple things in life the way Noah did.

She loved the man more than she wanted to admit. Sam mused over their relationship and how odd being with Noah was at times.

Oh, she knew the passion was there. She felt his tense body every time he held her in his arms. Even so, Noah always stopped short of taking the culmination of their love any further.

Throughout the day, she cooked and straightened up her apartment. This would be the first time they'd shared a meal in the apartment. Usually, they stayed downstairs in the inn, and would have coffee or tea after their dates, but never a meal, with the exception of Noah's subs.

The day had turned out to be cold. Sam had decided to wear a long skirt with a crew neck sweater.

At three in the afternoon, Noah knocked. Sam rushed to open the door. Standing there, Noah extended his hand that held a bouquet of fall flowers.

Sam gave him a once over. She smiled with satisfaction as she eyed his shirt that represented all the tale-tale signs of being new.

Noah's vision followed Sam's body and lingered in several places. "Sam, you look beautiful today." Making a stance of pretending to be taller, he straightened. "Do you think I fit in with a city girl?"

Sam placed a finger on her lip and inhaled a breath. "Hmmmm..."

She searched Noah up and down as she continued the fun banter. "Oh yes, I think you'll do extremely well." With a laugh, she motioned him into the living room. "Come on. I have everything finished."

Noah walked in the living area as aromas seeped into his nostrils. "The food smells good."

"Noah, it's chilly. Would you put more wood on the fire? I'll set the table."

Noah bent down to put a log on the fire. "I'm starved." Then without hesitation, he rose and firmly decreed, "Come here, Sam."

Curiously, she walked to him and stood in front of the crackling heat. Noah kissed her with a passion he couldn't deny. As her held her in his arms, he momentarily forgot what he was going to say.

Sam responded as her libido peaked with desire. Slowly, she ran her hands down his pristine shirt. "Noah, if I don't let go now, I might not be able to leave your arms."

Noah managed between the kisses to respond, "Yeah, I know. It sure is hard not to take you in my arms and whisk you off to the bedroom."

Sam tried to focus her mind. Confusion sounded in her voice as she responded. "Hum... I've wondered about that...I mean why you haven't tried to."

Noah stepped back and witnessed the questions in her eyes. "I want to very much, Sam. I thought you realized." Softening his voice, he explained, "You know I try to live a life that will please God, but that doesn't mean I don't suffer all the cravings that any flesh and blood man has. Honey, I yearn to be with you."

Rubbing his face with his hand, he continued. "Before I became a Christian, I did things that I know I shouldn't have. Now, I try my hardest to keep my faith. I want to wait on that special woman. The one the Lords wants me to spend my life with."

Noah held on to her hands as he tried to make her understand. "I've made mistakes, probably a lot, and I have to go to the Lord about them, but I try my best each day."

She grinned and pulled him back into her arms, molding his body against hers like a dangling carrot. "I understand that, Noah, but I need you."

Running a hand through her hair, he pulled her even tighter against his body. "I need you too, honey."

As he held her, she licked her lips and challenged him. "Noah, remember the story Pastor Stevens told in church? He said we all make mistakes and we receive forgiveness for them."

He took a shaky breath, his throaty gruff voice sounding in the air. "Yes, Sam—we can and we do. Nevertheless, I don't think God's happy about some of the choices people have made."

Sam stared into his eyes with longing and started a trail of kisses from his neck that led to his lips. She consumed them with a passion that needed no more words.

Both were lost in hunger, moaning filled the room. A sound of a knock on the door intruded and broke the mood between them.

Noah whispered to her between labored breaths. "Who is that? Are you expecting anyone?"

Sam backed out of his arms as her tingling lips rejected the disturbance. "No, let me see who's at the door and get rid of them."

Sam opened the door to find Pastor Stevens. He smiled at her as he held out a pie. "Hello Sam, how are you doing?" He peered behind Sam and nodded his head toward Noah, who stood behind Sam. "I just wanted to stop by and say Happy Thanksgiving and extend a dinner invitation. The misses wanted me to bring this pumpkin pie over and invite you to eat with us."

Sam felt like a cat caught with a bird in her mouth, even if she hadn't done what she was thinking. She stumbled for the words. "Uh...thank you Pastor, but I cooked for Noah and me."

John Stevens remained in the doorway. A smile continued to shine from his face. "I smelled your turkey at the door. The aroma is delicious, Sam."

She invited him in and listened as he spoke of the big turkey and all the trimmings that waited for him at home. Finally, he glanced at his watch and excused himself. With a quick goodbye, he was gone.

Shutting the door, Sam whirled around to Noah. She leaned against the door and nervously laughed. "Noah, I think God was watching us. He sent the Pastor by."

Joining in on the laugh, he replied, "I told you the Lord works things out in his own way."

The sound of Sam's voice turned serious. "Well, you remember what I just said—maybe I didn't have such a good idea."

Rubbing his hand through his hair, Noah looked deeply into her eyes. "Oh, you had a great idea, honey. Really, Sam, I hope you realize now how much I want you. I've fought with my urges for months." He remembered what he needed to ask her. "Sam, I have something I want to say and I can't wait any longer."

She observed him with interest as he guided her to the couch.

Sam paid close attention as he knelt down on one knee in front on her. Her hand flew to her mouth as the knowledge of what he was doing dawned of her.

Noah fiddled inside his pocket and finally he pulled out a small gold box.

Sam gaped at the velvet square while he took out a pear-shaped diamond that rested on a wide, white gold band.

Noah slid the band on her finger. "Sam, will you be my wife?"

She inhaled a deep breath as her heart leapt in answer. "My goodness, yes! I'll be your wife."

Eyeing the pear-shaped gem, she couldn't believe Noah had asked her to marry him. "Noah, this ring is beautiful."

As he witnessed Sam's smile, he knew he'd picked out the right ring. "I love you and want you to be Mrs. Noah Frye."

After dinner, they sat in front of the fire. Sam watched the yellow and red flames licking and listened to the wood pop. Cuddled on the sofa together, they talked about how they hoped their married life would be.

Noah took on a solemn face as he turned to face Sam. "What about the wedding date?"

She leaned against Noah. Not wanting to give into fear, she really didn't know what to say. "Women have to think about these kinds of things, Noah. I don't want to pull a date out from anywhere."

"Okay Sam, but don't take too much time. Every moment I'm without you, I question my sanity. I've waited so long for you."

Lying in bed that night Sam prayed. She poured out her heart to God and asked him to guide them to the truth so she would be free to be Noah's wife.

Noah returned to his house. His phone was beeping a message left from Belle.

After he returned Belle's call, he paced the floor, hardly able to contain his emotions. Doubt and questions plagued his thoughts.

He mentally sorted through events for the next hour—they weren't making sense. Nevertheless, he had to talk to Uncle Frank.

This situation needed checked out before he could say anything to anyone. He wouldn't make such accusations lightly.

Noah knew his uncle was out of town for the holiday and had informed him he wouldn't be reachable. So he called his home phone and left a message—all he could do for now.

Sunday morning came and Noah picked up Sam as usual. Before the service was over, he announced to the congregation that he had asked her to be his wife.

After the service, the pastor congratulated him. "I'm glad you and Sam found each other, with God's help of course. When will the wedding be?"

Noah gave the pastor a discouraged glance. "I couldn't say. You need to talk to the bride to be about that—seems she has to make a big deal out of picking a day."

The pastor's face lit with a grin. "Women are like that."

Noah agreed and added, "I suspect she's also worried about the trial."

Pastor Stevens offered a slight smile while he shook his head. "You know everyone in church is praying. We have to believe that God will find a way."

Sam and Noah headed out to the SUV with congratulations from all. As she stood in the churchyard, thinking about her pending wedding day, Belle jogged up to Sam and Noah.

Noah received a light hug with a friendly wink while she congratulated him.

As some young people pulled Noah to the side, Sam talked to Belle. "Would you be my maid of honor?"

"Sam, you know I will. When's the wedding going to be?"

Sam let out a sigh of frustration—she had to answer that same question all morning.

"I haven't picked out a day yet. I want everything perfect . I think I may tell Noah I want to wait until after the trial."

Belle searched Sam's face with marked pause. "Well, I'll be there for you. Just let me know."

That afternoon, Sam told Noah she wasn't attending night service.

"Are you sure you don't want to go to church tonight, Sam?"

She slightly grinned and shook her head no. "I want to stay home this evening. I'm really just stressed and want to be alone." Sam needed to straighten things out in her mind. Where was her life going? Should she add wedding plans to her list of things to worry about now?

As Noah kissed her goodbye for the evening, she noticed Anne's Christmas gift sitting on the entryway table. "Noah, would you take Anne's gift to her for me? I've been trying to get some presents handed out and haven't had a chance to go by Anne's house."

"If you want me to, I will. I planned on going to see her anyway."

Sam picked up the gift and handed the long box to him.

Noah grabbed the present as he placed quick kiss on Sam's lips. "Okay, I will see you sometime tomorrow."

Pulling into Anne's drive, Noah noticed the opening to her front porch roped off. Someone had been painting the house.

Eagerly, he walked to the back where he spotted Anne closing the garage door. Noah raised his voice a bit to get Anne's attention.

Anne jerked at the surprise of someone in her backyard and quickly latched the entranceway. "Noah, hi! It's good to see you."

As Anne approached Noah, they chatted about the holidays. Then Noah said, "Sam wanted me to bring this Christmas gift to you."

An unsure expression reached her eyes. "Sam got me a Christmas gift? But isn't it somewhat early?"

"Not really, Anne. There are just a few weeks left until Christmas. Sam doesn't know what Christmas week will hold, so she wanted to give out a few presents ahead of time."

Anne stared at Noah. "No, I bet not."

Something about the tone in Anne's voice brought out the protectiveness in him. "Anne, is there something about Sam you don't like?"

Anne slightly grinned. "Noah, I like her okay. I just have trouble getting to know people sometimes and you younger generations are always up to something new."

Silently, he stood there trying to figure out what Anne meant. Glancing around, he noticed her back deck had a fresh coat of paint on the banisters. Determined to change the subject, he motioned toward her deck. "I see you've done some painting around here."

Anne's focus followed Noah's direction. "Yes, I needed to repaint the outside."

Noah scanned the work and surveyed the paint. "The new paint has really made a difference, Anne. You picked a nice color."

Pushing his shoe around the grass, Noah decided to tell Anne about him and Sam. "Sam and I are getting married."

Anne stared at Noah oddly. Her voice got a little quieter. "What did you say? I mean, do you think that is a wise idea? With the murder and trial?"

"Anne, I don't care about that. I believe everything will work out. You know how long I've asked God to bring someone in my life. I believe Sam is the one. I think the Lord guided Bo to leave the inn to her so we could be together."

Treating Noah like a child, Anne uttered, "I don't want to upset you, of course. But Noah, you deserve to have a happy life and you ought to consider what will happen when she goes to jail."

Not if—*when*.

A surge of anger flared up. He gritted his teeth then forced himself to take a calming breath. Remembering Anne was older, he shoved a lid on his momentary irritation. "I can't believe for one minute that Sam killed anybody. When we get past this, we're going to be married."

Anne's mouth twisted. "So you haven't set a date?"

Noah hesitated before replying. "Not yet. Sam wanted to wait a while longer, but I want her to be my wife no matter what. I had hoped you would come to the wedding, Anne."

Anne played with the bow on the gift. "I didn't mean to sound ugly. I just want the best for you—for both of you. Of course, I will be there if there's a wedding."

If. That word bugged Noah all the way home.

In the middle of the week, Noah took Sam to dinner. Sam noticed Noah appeared distracted. "Sam, have you talked to my uncle?"

Sam put her fork down. "No, I haven't. I tried to call, but he was still out of town. Why Noah, what's wrong?"

Noah mouthed something she couldn't make out then said, "I have something to talk over with him."

As Sam watched Noah's face, the oddest sensation washed over her. "Is something wrong?"

Noah stopped eating. He really didn't want to have this conversation, but also he couldn't hurt Sam's feeling. "I spoke to someone a few nights ago and was told several things that I need to share with Uncle Frank."

Sam's curiosity peaked. "So what do you have to talk to him about?"

Noah sat beside her in silence a couple seconds and attempted to hide the sound of regret in his voice. "Sam, I can't say anything until I talk to Uncle Frank. It might be nothing."

When they arrived back at Sam's place, she went into the kitchen to retrieve a beverage then announced to Noah, "We need to talk. One thing we haven't gone over is where we are going to live."

Without any hesitation, he said, "Sam, I just assumed you wanted to stay here."

Sam turned and faced Noah, her face lit up. An air of happiness played in her eyes. "Yes Noah, I'd like to very much. But I want you to be happy about the place we call home."

Sounding final, he responded, "No problem. I've always liked this apartment. We can extend out. Maybe add a wraparound porch downstairs. With the proper roof built on, we can put an additional room up here if need be."

Sitting down her glass, Sam laid her arm on the back of the couch and visualized what he said. "Wow, my head is spinning. You've done some thinking about this."

He reached for Sam's hand and rubbed her fingers. "I've thought about it a time or two. This is your home now. I just rent. I certainly don't mind living here with you."

"All those plans sound great, Noah, but extra money is needed for renovating. Don't you think we might have to wait a while?"

Noah concentrated affectionately on Sam's ring finger. "Sam, we can afford it. I have the money. There was a small inheritance from Bo—and he always wanted to put a wraparound porch on the inn.

"Through the years, I've invested also. The money should be put to good use. When we get married, we can have some plans drawn up. Then you can see what the inn would look like if it was updated."

Sam watched him intently. "I believe I would like to remodel, but that's your money."

"No, it will be money for our family. I just assumed you wanted a family one day."

Sam knew the answer in her heart. She had always hoped to have a child one day—she could easily picture a little curly-haired Noah underfoot.

She tossed her head back and the sparkle in her eyes told him all he needed to know. Before Noah left, he conned a promise out of Sam. Now she had to think about a wedding date.

He even suggested they marry before the first of the year, so they could start the New Year off together as man and wife.

She would not break a promise, especially not to Noah. She had spent most of her time thinking about the court date—not too much bearing had been put into her wedding. Sam was sure about this one thing—she wanted to be Mrs. Noah Frye.

As she got ready for bed, she talked to the Lord. Her emotions pulled back and forth and she wondered how they could get married before the first of the New Year. For the next hour, she lay in bed and tossed. She knew she would have to rely on God to make the marriage possible for them.

The next week flew by fast. Sam tried to keep herself busy. December was supposed to be a festive, happy month, but she couldn't help but worry.

She never did find out what Noah wanted to speak to his uncle about. She was just glad that Mr. Cane had returned from his trip.

On Wednesday afternoon, Noah called to say he couldn't pick her up for church because he had to meet with his uncle. He typically went to service on Wednesday night, but he wasn't saying anything specific and Sam knew whatever they were doing had to be important.

She couldn't help but worry and wonder if everything was all right and what had him so distracted again.

CHAPTER TWELVE

After her morning coffee, Sam rushed to answer the phone to find Mr. Cane on the line. "Sam, I've talked to Sheriff Gruver about the older model truck. He didn't have much to say, but he assured me he planned to check into things.

"I've also worked on some other angles of your case. Certain situations have come to my attention and I hope the sheriff can track down the answers for us."

Sam couldn't help but wonder why Mr. Cane was being very vague—as was Noah. "What is he checking into, Mr. Cane? Will it prove I didn't kill anyone?"

"I—" Frank's voice wavered before he spoke. "We just have to wait and see Sam. It may turn this case around. I really don't want to say much at this point. It could damage reputations and friendships unnecessarily. When I have all the facts on my desk, then we'll know more.

"Sam, one more thing—if you see that truck parked across from the inn again, even briefly, I want you to be sure to call the police. This is important."

Sam slammed the phone receiver down, narrowing her eyes. She fussed at herself for not speaking up—after all this was her life.

What had Mr. Cane found? She picked up the receiver to call him back, armed with a mouthful of things she planned to say to the man. Then, with a second thought, she slowly put the phone down. Whatever he was working on sounded positive for her case. She would let it go for now. The tone of the conversation and the promise of more evidence did sound good and made her feel better.

She went into the bedroom. She couldn't explain her why, but for some reason that phone call had sparked a new hope. Her mind jumped back to what Noah had said about a wedding date.

Sam remembered she'd seen a bridal shop at the mall. In an instant, she made a snap decision and announced aloud, "I'm going to the mall. It's time I bought a wedding dress and put my faith into action."

As she dressed, Sam also decided that December twenty-sixth was the day she wanted to become Noah's wife. The church would still have some poinsettias sitting around and the bright Christmas colors would make it more festive. She hummed a tune the choir had sung in church Sunday as she headed down the road toward the shopping center.

Not long after, Sam stood at the entrance of the dress shop, her eyes darting from a rack full of white gowns to all the other displays.

While she meandered down the aisles, she reflected on everything that had the changed in her life. This time last year, she couldn't even imagine the need to buy a wedding dress.

A sales clerk approached and interrupted her thoughts. "Can I help you find something?"

"I am looking for a dress, maybe something with an A-line."

The saleslady guided Sam across the room to a wall that was covered with dresses in the style that she'd been thinking of. "You let me know if you want to try any on."

Two hours later, Sam had made her decision. As she stood at the counter and paid for the dress, she had to admire the design. It wasn't as fancy as most of the dresses in the store, but Sam had fallen in love with it as soon as the saleslady showed it to her.

She finally had her wedding dress—an A-line with long sleeves and an off-the-shoulder neckline. Satin and white beads detailed the sleeves and hem.

To her, this was the prettiest dress she had ever seen. Of course, she tried on a lot more elaborate dresses, but this was the one for her. The size and fit were perfect. She just felt right in it...and ready to become Noah's wife.

Carefully, Sam placed the dress in the trunk and scooted in her seat. She clicked the seatbelt around her and started her engine as she checked the rearview mirror to see if she was safe to back out of the parking spot.

Immobilized in her spot, her heart raced. Fear tightened around her throat and tried to choke her. A sudden sickness pushed up from the pit of her stomach. Behind her, a man stood in front of the theater. From the distance, she couldn't be one-hundred percent sure, but it looked to be Rob.

Her hand shook as she shifted gears, determined to kept the man in view. Was it really him? Had he followed her here?

With a roar, she shifted her VW into drive and sped out. Her mind painted a vision of him barreling down on her.

She was sure now that he'd followed her to Big Fork. How, she wondered, did he find her? She didn't tell anyone where she was going.

All the way home, she searched her mirrors and peeped back and forth, but not once did she spot his old truck—maybe she had escaped without him seeing her.

Ordering herself to calm down, Sam concentrated on calling Mr. Cane the moment she returned home.

Later that night, after Sam had napped and showered, she checked to make sure that the old truck wasn't parked anywhere. Then she trotted downstairs to work on some of accounts and ads for the inn.

She had called Noah after her conversation with Mr. Cane and told him about Rob. He'd offered to come over and stay, even suggesting he bunk down on her couch for the night.

The idea of having Noah spend the night brought all sorts of fantasies to her mind, but she only wanted him staying for the right reasons.

She didn't want him to feel as if he had to be her protector all the time.

Sam stood her ground, persistent in not wanting to have company. She assured him she had work to do and would be okay.

Now Sam sat in her office with a stack of papers. Thoughts started to parade through her mind and fought to pull her away from the peace she was determined to have.

Taking a slow breath, she opened her desk and pulled out her notepad. One thing she had discovered while living in Big Fork Lake was if she stayed busy, then she had less time to wallow in self-pity.

With pen in hand, she planned her future. She tapped her lips with the pen as she concentrated on the things she needed to do for her wedding. On the last page of her notebook, she jotted down part of the Serenity Prayer. *God grant me the courage to accept the things I cannot change and the wisdom to know the difference...*

After going into the kitchen to make coffee, she returned to her desk, mentally going over the details for the wedding.

She knew Noah wanted to have the wedding at the church. She had talked to Pastor Stevens earlier about the date. He had assured her he could marry them December twenty-sixth.

Pastor Stevens' wife said Belle would help her with the decorations and reception after the service. The church had music for the ceremony. Sam's only request was that they keep the event small.

All she needed to do for that day was to get her hair done and arrive at the church. Providing she was still a free woman.

Laying her pen down, Sam twisted her mouth in thought. Bowing her head she prayed, knowing only God could change things.

Speaking aloud, she asked God to guide them and help her find the truth. "I trust you Lord. I want a new start this New Year with Noah as my husband."

On Saturday, December seventeenth, Noah called and asked Sam if he could bring over Chinese.

"Sure, that would be great. There's something I need to tell you anyway. I've waited long enough. "

The way Sam made that comment puzzled Noah—he started wondering what was wrong. "Is everything okay, Sam?"

"Yes, I've made a decision, that's all. I need to tell you."

Noah's chest tensed and he massaged a foreseen headache, concerned at what she had on her mind. "Sam, you're scaring me."

"Don't be scared, silly. Just come over."

All afternoon, Noah speculated about what Sam had to tell him. He realized the time was getting close to the court date. He only hoped whatever she had on her mind didn't have anything to do with the trial.

The last thing Noah wanted was to lose Sam. No matter what it took or which way things turned out, he was sure he loved Sam and wanted her to be his wife.

CHAPTER THIRTEEN

Noah arrived thirty minutes before he was supposed to and immediately took her into his arms. "Sorry I'm early, Sam. I just couldn't wait any longer to see you." Noah released Sam and gazed into her eyes for any signs of sadness. He handed her the food.

All day, he had imagined different scenarios as to what tonight held for his and Sam's future. It wasn't like him to stress, but even though he had gone to God and prayed Sam wasn't thinking about doing anything stupid, he worried. She meant so much to him.

She smiled at him as she placed the takeout on the table. "I'll get some plates for the food. You sit down."

While dishing out the food, Noah remarked, "Sam please, will you tell me what is going on?"

Seated beside him, she gauged his reaction. "Nothing Noah, I've just decided that I want to marry you on December twenty-sixth."

Noah's mouth was parted with a fork full of rice almost at his lips. The weight of Sam's words knocked the food off his fork, causing a spill. "The twenty-sixth?"

He reached over and locked her in his embrace, smothering his nose in her hair. "Sam, that's great. Whatever day you want. I just can't wait until we can be man and wife."

They spent the rest of the evening engaged in conversation about the wedding, discussing the things on Sam's list they needed to accomplish. As the night moved in, Sam reluctantly led him to the door.

Noah paused in the threshold. He didn't want to leave, but at least she had set a wedding date. Soon, she would be his and he could stay right where he belonged—in her home, her heart, her bed.

Holding her close, he pulled her body to him. He let his mouth travel hotly down to the base of her throat. His husky voice flowed in deep breaths. "Sam, I want to stay with you tonight."

As usual, a river of longing flowed inside and caused heat to rise all the way to the top of her head. Wasn't that what she wanted also?

Embraced in his arms, she held back. Despite the desire that ran rampant throughout her body, she moved out of his arms. It took all her fortitude to gather courage to say no.

The months of listening to the things Noah had said played in her mind like a movie. He did make sense. She was God's child now.

She realized that she wanted to start her marriage out fresh, with Noah and with God.

Gently, she kissed him and backed away. "Noah, I want you so much, but we'll wait."

After he left, Sam slumped down on the couch and watched her favorite television show. The next hour she slowly made her way to the bedroom. She moved to the window and stared out at the murky, cloudy night. If only the stars were shining brighter, she thought.

The night was cold and she gazed toward the street. She might not have noticed otherwise, but the wind blew and tossed the Big Fork Inn & Eats sign, the movement causing her to eyes to wonder to the far end of the road. There, perched in the darkness, appeared to be a familiar object.

She squinted and tried to focus on the spot. What was out there?

The clouds moved just long enough for her to distinguish the silhouette of a vehicle. The truck blended into the trees, camouflaged against the shadowy night.

Her heart thumped and a gasp escaped her suddenly dry lips. Hard flutters beat in her chest as she stared out the window.

She stood paralyzed, unsure of what she needed to do. She remained motionless, staring out the window while the fear mocked her.

The more her eyes lingered on the odd-looking spot, the more assured she was that it was the same black vehicle that had spied on her all these months.

Clearing her head, Sam took a hard breath and remembered what Mr. Cane had asked her to do. Forcing herself not to run, she slowly turned away and headed toward the phone.

"Sheriff Gruver! That truck is parked at the far end of the parking lot!"

"Sam, calm down. You just stay away from the windows. I'll have my deputy ride out your way. He's close to the area anyway."

With shaky hands, Sam pushed the button down on the phone. It took her two attempts but she was finally able to punch in Noah's phone number. "Noah, I saw Rob's truck parked across the street again."

Noah listened to Sam's voice laced with apprehension. Immediately, he started to pull on his shoes.

"I'll drive out toward the inn, honey. You go to bed, get some rest. Leave this to the sheriff. And Sam?"

"Yes?"

"I'm here for you. He will not hurt you again."

She hung up the phone, seriously doubting sleep would ever come to her tonight.

Ten minutes later, Noah scrutinized the side of the road that lay just ahead in his view. He'd pulled off the street, not wanting the stalker to see him approach.

Positioned beside the truck, the deputy questioned the driver. Parked in an obscure location, Noah searched out the shadows and examined the exchange.

He desperately wished he could catch sight of whoever was behind the wheel. An old saying of Bo's popped in his mind and he blurted it in the mist of his cab. "I sure would love to be a fly on the wall."

After ten minutes, Noah decided to head home. Whatever was going on, the deputy was taking his own sweet time. Meddling wouldn't help Sam's case anyway.

The week she'd dreaded all these months finally came. That Tuesday morning the telephone rang out, breaking into Sam's morning routine. Mr. Cane spoke in a hurry. "Sam dear, I hope you're not too stressed about the trial."

Dread clamped on to Sam. The trial had been the only thing on her mind for days.

She rubbed her head, fending off a headache. "Mr. Cane, I'm trying to stay calm. I'm just so worried. What if they find me guilty?"

"Sam, your case looks better. Things have turned around in your favor. We just need to get your day in court over with so you and Noah can begin your lives together."

As Sam listened to Mr. Cane, she felt a spark of hope. His hurried speech was hard to follow, but he did tell her that a new development had happened, and he was on his way to find all the details out.

Mr. Cane proceeded to talk, making a few comments Sam couldn't figure out. Finally, he asked, "Do you want me to drive you to the courthouse?"

Wiping her fingers across her left eye, she responded, "No. Thank you anyway, but Noah is picking me up."

Responding immediately, he said, "Okay Sam, I'll see you Thursday morning at nine."

Sam stood in her spot and mulled over the things Mr. Cane had relayed. She prayed that this new development would set her free.

Sam started to walk off when the phone sounded again.

Picking up the receiver again, she grinned as she heard Noah's greeting on the other end of the line. "Hi Sam, how are you this morning?"

She sat down on the couch and found herself contemplating how Noah had an easy-going way about him. "Your uncle just called and said my case looked better. I believe he's found something that will help my case."

"What all did he say, Sam?"

"Not really a lot, but he did say some new developments in the case have turned up and he was checking into them. I hope everything is all right."

"I'm sure everything is fine. He was probably just busy. I hope whatever he's working on ends this whole mess for us. Well, I have a job that needs to be inspected. I just wanted to speak to my favorite lady. I love you."

"I love you too, Noah."

Sam hung up phone. Her nerves crawled as she inwardly imagined what things might be going on. As she struggled over the next few hours to keep herself busy, she wondered why she had such an unsettled feeling.

Was it that she feared the unknown or the anticipation of something good?

Meanwhile, across town in the sheriff's office, the day started out in a rush. By late evening, Sheriff Gruver read over his file as he mentally pieced together a picture of a disturbed person. He paced his office, rubbed his coarse jaw whiskers and thought of the years he'd been on the police force of Big Fork Lake.

Nothing like this had ever happened before and the turn of events this case uncovered shocked him.

Earlier in the interrogation room, he hadn't made any sense out of what had been said. He finally got aggravated talking in the same circles and figured a night in the cell might make things clearer in the morning.

While he waited on his deputy to return from the search, he reread his notes in an attempt to sort things out.

The sheriff's door opened and the deputy hiked in. "Sheriff, we found a patch of yew berry bushes in the backyard beside the garage and these in the freezer on the back porch."

Sheriff Gruver stared at a garbage bag full of Top's warehouse containers as his second in command asked, "What do you want to do now?"

The big man went to his coat rack and reached for his coat. "I'm going home for the night. Tomorrow morning we'll get to the bottom of this."

Sam waved goodbye to Noah as he backed out of the parking lot of the inn. Earlier, he'd taken her to a nice restaurant in Montgomery where they enjoy a five-star meal.

While she got ready for bed, she went over her earlier conversation with Mr. Cane. That morning he told her that the case was looking better, but this afternoon he hadn't offered her any indication that anything positive had surfaced. Why was he so closemouthed? The trial was scheduled in two days. She needed to know *something*. Wasn't that her right?

After breakfast, the sheriff presided at the head of the long table in the small room he used to question people and narrowed his eyes toward the other end.

"I don't like this a bit. I know you planned this. The only way for me to help you is if you come clean. I need to be told everything."

The cold, calculated response shocked Sheriff Gruver. "Humph! You *know* I had to do it. You can see that, can't you?"

He straddled the chair as his mind toiled to make sense what was happening. "No, you did not. You killed an innocent man. That's murder."

The tap-tap of a foot pecked against the floor. The noise drew his attention as he stared into the hard-edged expression and listened to the grudging voice. "That Sam had this coming. She rightfully should be the one blamed for this. The only reason I *had* to do something was because she meddled into everything."

The big man leaned back in his chair. All his years in law enforcement didn't prepare him for a situation such as this. He thought he knew this woman. Liked her. He sat in his chair and wondered how much more he could stomach of her mixed-up conversation.

Sheriff Gruver raised his voice. "What are you talking about? None of this has anything to do with the fact that we found the pies Samantha Blacker ordered in your freezer and I know you're the one who made the poisoned pie that killed a man. What is this all about, Anne?"

The answer came with a puff of air. Hands swayed to make a point.

"She wasn't what she should've been. That woman took advantage of *everybody*. She's not the kind that belongs here. She should go back to Atlanta."

With a huff of disappointment, Sheriff Gruver tossed a harsh glance at the stiff stance of the older woman.

Anne's unyielding body scooted closer to the edge of her seat.

"I only did what I needed to do. Sam changed everything. It was my place to protect Bo's inn. He would have wanted things to stay the way they were. She shouldn't have come to Big Fork Lake."

Sheriff Gruver took in her odd demeanor. He definitely faced a very strange situation indeed. "Anne, will you tell me what happened?"

Carefully she placed her hands on the table and cleared her throat as she started to speak. "All I wanted was for her to leave. We were fine before she showed up. Bo told me once that I could even make poison taste good. I guess I did huh, Sheriff?" As if she were a broken record, she repeated herself. "I needed to protect Bo's inn."

Even though he had known Anne for ten years, he was the Sheriff of Big Fork Lake, Alabama and would do what was right. "All right Anne, go on. Tell me the rest."

She focused on the floor while she recapped her side of the events. "After Sam went up to her apartment that evening, I took out the pies and put them in a trash bag. When everything was clear, I toted them to my car. I wasn't serving pre-made food in *my* diner."

Anne's next words were harsh, more to herself than to the sheriff. "I should have tossed them out. I just didn't want anyone to find those stupid pies, so I was afraid to move them."

Focusing on the badge on his chest, she continued. "When I got home, I crammed them in my freezer. Then I remembered what Bo said to me one time. So I went out in my yard and picked some berries and I made a pie. After it cooled, I carried it back to the inn."

Sheriff Gruver took a slow breath and patiently asked, "Anne, what was Sam doing at this time?"

Anne smiled and curtly remarked, "Oh, I didn't have to worry about her. I sent her up to the apartment earlier with a glass of tea. I put two sleeping pills in her drink. She would have slept through anything. Only while I was there, Mr. Brookshire came in. He wanted a slice of pie too. I planned to save it for Sam, but I figured this would work also.

"If Sam was in trouble, she would tuck her tail and run back to Atlanta where she belonged." Anne jerked her head and faced the wall. "Sheriff, I didn't mean to kill him, just make him sick, but he insisted on having two slices of pie. I was proud of that pie."

A change of expression crossed her face as she looked at Sheriff Gruver with an accusation. "I still figured I'd give her some of that dessert, but you arrested her. I ended up having to pretend to drop it on the floor when that scatterbrain Belle wanted a slice."

Thursday morning came—the day of the trial. Sam stared out the window in despair. Her stomach sloshed around from too much coffee and not enough sleep.

She never could find out if Mr. Cane had any good news. The last time she talked to him, he said he was still waiting on the sheriff to send him the report he needed. He apologized to her and said he couldn't explain anything until he knew all the facts.

She tried to center her attention on the night before. Noah had come over and she'd cooked a special dinner for them.

Sam speculated if it would prove to be the last meal she could prepare for a while.

Warmness crept inside her as she directed her thoughts to his goodnight kiss. How she bathed in the comfort of his arms.

She wanted to remember that feeling just in case it was the last time he circled her in an embrace.

Noah headed to his door to leave when his phone rang. Thinking it was Sam on the phone, he hurried to pick up the receiver.

"Uncle Frank, huh, what did you say? When did you find out? I can't wait to tell Sam."

Disappointment caught Noah as his uncle informed him not to repeat anything. The judge was still working on the particulars and even though his uncle was hopeful as to what was going to happen, he just didn't know if the case would be resolved today. "Noah, it's best if we wait until we get in the courtroom. The pending charges aren't official yet—matters could still go either way. I just wanted to fill you in on some of the details. I know Sam is upset. I thought it would help you keep her in a positive mood if you knew her case will most likely be dismissed."

At eight o'clock, Noah arrived at Sam's to take her to the courthouse. "Sam, are you ready to go?"

Standing there stuck to one spot, her insides rumbled, sweat beaded up on her palms, and she fought hard to keep her nerves at bay. "I'm just a nervous wreck."

Noah moved to hold Sam in his arms. With all his will, he attempted to calm her while he fought against his loyalty to his uncle.

Words he needed to say hung on the tip of his tongue. He opened his mouth and started to tell her what he'd learned as guilt pricked his soul and forced him to remember the promise he made.

His heart ripped in two—all he could do for now was offer her comfort and assurance that everything was going to be all right.

"Sam, honey, I know. But please believe me, everything has been worked out. Everything will be okay."

Sam shot an unconvinced look toward him and pushed out of his arms. "Noah. How do you know that?"

Noah surrounded Sam again in a tight cuddle and felt her body as she sank into his embrace. "I know God has guided my uncle to the truth, Sam. Please, trust me on this."

As they walked out the door, Sam silently wished she was as sure as Noah that things would be all right.

Mr. Cane stood waiting on the top step of the courthouse.

Sam huddled with her head down close to her coat collar. She wasn't sure if the wind made her cold or if the bitterness of the day caused her to shiver.

Frank's head moved back and forth as he glanced at them both. "Sam, you're not looking too well today."

Sam stopped suddenly on the steps. "Gee, thanks Mr. Cane, but what do you expect?"

Mr. Cane ignored her tone and smiled as he replied, "I expect you are going to be pleased."

Sam lifted her face and threw him a puzzled stare. "Why would I be pleased? I'm going to trial for a murder I didn't commit."

Frank pretended not to hear Sam's remark and turned to Noah. "I kind of figured you wouldn't be able to keep quiet, but I was wrong."

Noah gazed at Sam with a regretful expression as he remarked, "It was hard, Uncle Frank, but I promised I wouldn't."

Sam's mouth flew open and she stared at the men in unbelief. Mounting with frustration, her eyes pierced them with arrows.

She could swear she saw a quick smile flash across Mr. Cane's lips.

Her pulse raced while she gritted her teeth with annoyance. "This is not the time for games. What's going on Mr. Cane? I demand to know. Now!"

"Sam, I'm sorry but this can't be talked about yet. We don't want to be late for court. Trust me. Your case has been sorted out. After this, I'll tell you the whole story."

While Sam followed them into the courtroom, her legs bounced as if they were rubber bands. She focused on the old pictures of Congress to keep her emotions steady.

Her head was spinning with different scenarios. Definitely, she was concerned about what lie ahead, but for some reason, though she wanted to get this over with, she was no longer scared.

Her gut told her something was going on and it was good. She trusted both Mr. Cane and Noah and they seemed to feel as if everything was going to turn out right for her in the end.

With court called to order, the judge scanned all the faces before he spoke. "Mr. Cane, I have the confession in hand. I also have spoken to Sheriff Gruver and considering the new facts that have transpired over the past couple days, I see no reason for this to continue."

Frank turned slightly in Sam's direction and a brief smile crossed his face. "Thank you, sir. I motion for the court to dismiss the charges against my client, Samantha Blacker."

The judge scanned his file before he responded. "Yes, Mr. Cane, I concur with you."

He turned his attention to Sam. "Ms. Blacker, the State has dismissed all charges against you. You are free to go. I hope you have a Merry Christmas."

Sam floated on knees that wanted to leap. She could hardly believe what she heard. Inside, she was jumping up and down, her emotions weaving back and forth from relief to excitement.

All she could do now was smile. She was free, her name cleared. She couldn't wait to get outside.

She couldn't wait to get married!

As they walked through the courthouse doors, the cool wind slapped Sam's face. She paid no attention to the air—all she could think about was the fact that her insurmountable problem was suddenly over.

Torn between yelling and crying for joy, she kept repeating to herself that she was free from the murder charges. *Free!*

Pivoting on the last step, Sam grabbed Frank and kissed him.

Noah tossed a giant-sized grin at Sam and in a light manner teased, "Hey now, wait a minute—you're marrying me, remember?"

Sam latched on to Noah with a kiss as a silent tear slid down her face. She turned to face Noah's uncle. "What happened? I can't wait to hear! How did you get the charges dropped, Mr. Cane?"

Frank Cane peered at Sam. In all his years as a lawyer, this was probably one of the few times he honestly delighted in the outcome of a case. "Let's go to my car and get out of this cool air so we can talk."

Settled in the car beside Noah, Sam listened as Frank recalled what transpired over the last two days, also explaining why he couldn't say anything until the last minute.

Sam sighed and spoke with sadness. "Instead, her pie killed him. Why did she do this, Mr. Cane?"

Soberly, he looked toward them and shook his head in dismay. "It's hard to tell. From what I've learned, she is a very confused woman. She convinced herself she was trying to keep the inn the way Bo would have wanted. She took the pies out of the freezer and tore up the invoice that came from the warehouse."

Sam sat between both men and listened in shock. She was happy to be free from the murder charge, but part of her heart reached out for Anne. "Noah, I feel so bad for her."

"At least it worked out and you're not going to jail for something she did. See Sam, God guided us to the truth. I knew he would."

The three of them went to the nearest restaurant and conversed further about the events that took place.

Sam glanced around, wrapped in the sensation of pleasure as she relaxed in her seat and enjoyed the conversation. Finally, she could talk about their wedding without fearing it wouldn't happen. This was the first time she could be totally happy and focused on her big day. She couldn't believe that in less than a week she would walk down the aisle.

Standing outside the restaurant some time later, Frank informed them that he would see them at church. Before he turned to leave, he took Sam's hand. "Sam, I want you to call me Frank. After all, we'll be family in a week."

Sam and Noah shopped the rest of the day for a tree and Christmas decorations to make the inn festive. In a fast decision, she planned a Christmas Eve party with the intention of inviting everyone she could think of to come.

She wanted all of Big Fork Lake to know the inn was a safe place to eat and stay.

They delighted in decorating and Noah made phone calls. He invited as many people as he could to help them celebrate the occasion.

"Noah, I've wanted to ask you something."

"Sure Sam, what's on your mind?"

She turned to face him and continued, "What had you so distracted and hurried to see your uncle a couple of weeks ago?"

Noah lowered his head in an apologetic gesture. "I wasn't able to say anything to you. Not until I talked to Uncle Frank, but Belle called and told me that she saw a yew tree in Anne's backyard. She said she believed that bush was the only one close by.

"That was what got Uncle Frank checking into Anne. He found out that she still owned her late husband's old black truck. Uncle Frank then called the sheriff and told him. They both checked into some things and waited for Anne to make a mistake."

Moving over to the tree, he placed an ornament on the branch and continued to talk. "When you called Sheriff Gruver about the truck parked at the end of your drive, they found Anne inside wrapped up in a blanket, watching you. When the deputy shined his flashlight inside her truck, he noticed a ripped up invoice from Top's Warehouse."

Sam stood mesmerized by the blinking lights around the tree as she listened. Automatically she said, "Then they found the pies in her freezer. I feel sorry for Anne."

Noah placed his arm around her waist and took hold of Sam's hand while he admired the tree. "I know. Anne is confused. Prayer is all we can do for her now."

Sam looked into her bathroom mirror at the last minute before she went downstairs. She was glad she purchased a couple of party dresses at The Bride Mart.

Yes, she definitely liked the royal blue, velvet chemise dress with the scoop neck and half sleeves. Sam twirled as she checked her image again. "I hope Noah likes my outfit. He's never seen me dressed up like this before," she commented to herself.

Noah opened the front door without knocking and entered the inn. His arms held bags that contained extra party supplies.

One look at Sam and his eyes popped. His face turned a shade of red.

He stood there briefly speechless and exhibiting all the signs of a man who appreciated a beautiful woman. Swallowing hard, Noah's voice cracked. "Sam, you're beautiful. Wow, I won't be able to keep my hands off you tonight. It was really good that you didn't dress like that before."

Sam laughed—that was exactly the reaction she wanted. Innocently, she remarked, "Why Noah?"

He wiggled his eyebrows up and down. "I would have needed to pray every minute just for the strength to keep from devouring you." Noah pulled her close and crushed the velvet dress against his body as he ran his hand along the soft material. "Are you all set for the wedding?"

Eagerness flooded her veins. *Yes, I'm ready! Of course, I can't wait.* Calmly, she responded, "I can't believe that in two days I will be Mrs. Noah Frye."

With the party in full swing, Belle walked up to Sam. "This is my cousin. She's the manager at the theater."

Sam shook the hand of a short, preppy-dressed woman who appeared to be ten years older than Belle. "Hi and thanks for giving Belle some work until she can come back."

The woman grinned. "I needed the extra help, especially around the holidays. I hate to see her go."

Sam peeped over at her young friend who wore her usual ponytail. "Well, I need her now. She's valuable around here."

With a face that held an agreeable smile, the shorter woman said, "I don't think she wanted to work at the theater anyway. For some reason, she likes this place. Excuse me ladies, I've got to find something to eat."

After she headed toward the counter, Sam turned to Belle and begun to enlighten her as to what she planned for the inn the next year.

"So we need to have a grand opening March first. I hoped I could count on you to help me get everything ready."

Belle flashed a grin, her face gleaming. "Sure Sam, I'll be glad to help you."

In approval, Sam announced, "I also need a manager for the inn. Will you be my manager?"

Belle studied what Sam said for only a second, her face shining even brighter. "I guess so...I mean, of course I will. You're not going to manage the place?"

Sam's hair swayed on her shoulders as she nodded rapidly. "No, I think I am going to concentrate on other things. I'll keep the books, order supplies and clean the cabins. I also need to set up a better filing system to track my orders and supplies that are delivered from this day forward."

"Everything will be all right around here from this point on."

"Belle, I believe God led me here to find my life—He has also shown me that no matter what might happen, I need to believe in his loving guidance. Anyway, I want you to take care of the everyday duties. That will leave me free for other things, if I want."

Belle mischievously added, "Like make a family?"

Sam smiled shyly. "I guess, we'll have to see."

Belle eagerly shook her head. "Okay, but Sam, remember I can't cook that good yet."

Remembering Belle's last attempt at making pastries, Sam laughed. "Don't worry about that. We'll have a decent cook hired before the season opens."

Sam glanced across the room and her bones chilled. She nudged Belle and asked, "Do you see that man over there?"

Belle followed her eyes in the direction of Sam's glare. "Are you talking about the one in the blue jean jacket?"

Unable to speak, Sam nodded her head in agreement.

"He is my cousin's husband. Why do you ask?"

Relief flooded her. "He just looks so much like someone I use to know."

With a quick glance toward the tables, Belle turned. "I'd better find my cousin. Have a good Christmas and I'll see you at church tomorrow."

From across the room, Sam watched as the sheriff of Big Fork Lake approached. Even with all she'd been through, inwardly she respected the big man. "I need to apologize to you, Sam, for the way I acted."

Sam gave an understanding nod. "You were just thinking of the town's best interest."

Accepting her politeness, he continued, "I was rude to you and wrong. I realize now that sometimes change can be a good thing. I'm glad you are calling Big Fork Lake your home and congratulations to you and Noah on your upcoming wedding."

Sam smiled, truly grateful. "Thank you, Sheriff. Hearing that means a lot to me. I hope you'll come to our wedding."

"I wouldn't miss your wedding, Sam. I know you and Noah will be happy. " He tipped his hat as he turned to walk away.

Noah slid up beside her with a glass of punch. "Hi, honey. What's wrong? You seem a bit jumpy."

Sam motioned toward the other side of the room. "Everything is okay now. I just saw someone who looked exactly like Rob. He must have been the man I saw at the mall."

Noah slid his hand in his pocket and rattled something. "That's over now. We've started a new life. As long as I am around nothing or no one will ever hurt you again."

Contentment washed over her. Indeed, she did have a fresh start and truly felt that with God and Noah on her side, matters would always work out for the good.

"Yes, you're right. We've begun a new life. Soon you'll be my husband. One day, maybe soon, we'll have some children."

Noah smiled with a resounding, "I hope so."

Sam watched as he pulled something out of his shirt pocket. "I want to give you something."

Her eyes darted to the box he held in his hand. "Christmas isn't until tomorrow."

Deep down inside she bubbled with excitement. The first Christmas gift of many more to come from the man I love, she thought.

Sam watched as he handed her a long container wrapped in red paper. She only hesitated a second before she opened it and slowly picked up a set of keys. Her eyes bulged as she held the key ring with a shiny red heart. "What's this, Noah?"

Noah leaned back on his heels. His face shined with satisfaction. "The keys to your new SUV."

She grabbed her mouth as a squeal of glee escaped her lips. "My SUV! You really mean it, Noah?"

The town folk cheered them on and watched as Noah kissed the hand that was holding the heart. "I purchased the SUV for you, Sam, and for our family."

"Oh Noah, I love you."

Noah wrapped his arms around Sam and whispered in her ear as applause and shouts of joy rang out in the inn.

"I promise to love you forever, Sam."

Standing there they embraced each other, swimming in their very own pool of love.

Silently, they sent up a private prayer of thanks to God. Sam moved slightly in Noah's arms and soaked in the look of love on his face. Almost shyly she said, "Thank you, Jesus, for your blessings on us."

Noah's smile widened as he added, "And your merciful grace and guidance." Clasping hands they both spoke, "That led to the truth and paved our futures."

ABOUT THE AUTHOR

Mary Lou Ball lives in North Carolina and writes novels and Christian articles. Her passion is weaving together inspirational romantic suspense and mysteries, which show the imperfect lives of everyday characters as they face hardships and struggles while discovering the real meaning of grace. Her books will encourage you to see the magic of love, hope and a divine guidance that often lies dormant, waiting to be found by each of us. When she's not writing she enjoys the outdoors, family and singing Gospel music with her husband. Some of her Christian Articles are found on Examiner.com at: http://www.examiner.com/christian-living-in-greensboro/mary-ball.

Learn more about Mary at http://MaryLouwrites.weebly.com.

Thank you for your purchase.

We hope you've enjoyed your read and invite you to visit us online for more sweet and inspirational romance titles from Inspired Romance Novels!

www.inspiredromancenovels.com

www.ingramcontent.com/pod-product-compliance
Lightning Source LLC
Chambersburg PA
CBHW071239130626
46556CB00003B/1076